Desiree

MY FUNNY VALENTINE

A Valentine's Novella

Blue Saffire

*With love,
Blue Saffire
aka
Royal
Blue*

Perceptive Illusions Publishing, Inc.
Bay Shore, New York

Blue Saffire/Perceptive Illusions Publishing, Inc.
PO BOX 5253
Bay Shore, New York 11706
www.BlueSaffire.com

Publisher's Note: This is a work of fiction. Names, characters, places, and incidents are a product of the author's imagination. Locales and public names are sometimes used for atmospheric purposes. Any resemblance to actual people, living or dead, or to businesses, companies, events, institutions, or locales is completely coincidental.

Ordering Information:
Quantity sales. Special discounts are available on quantity purchases by corporations, associations, and others. For details, contact the "Special Sales Department" at the address above.

My Funny Valentine/ Blue Saffire. -- 1st ed.
ISBN 978-1-941924-64-8

Love has no one color. Beauty has no one face.
-Blue Saffire

Musing

Nelson

Look at her. I've never seen a woman so full of life. Talina lights up a room from the moment she walks in. It's in her complete essence, from the way she walks to her sultry laugh, to the way her eyes light up with that same laugh.

Talina just moves in a way that grabs your attention, with little to no effort on her behalf. I wish I could find a woman like her to call my own. Sadly, she has been in a relationship, since she started working for my company and it has always been my policy not to date employees.

No, instead, I'm stuck dating the same shells over and over. Women that are no more attracted to me, than I am to them. Not that they aren't gorgeous women. No, I pull some of the finest. They just have no depth, not the kind of depth I'm looking for. Not what I need.

At thirty-eight, I need someone to compliment me and my accomplishments. It took me years to get here. I look around the ballroom of my company's holiday party. It's a big event for my marketing firm to kick off the holiday season, just before Thanksgiving.

Major clients flew out to see what my team has had up its sleeves. Thanks to minds like Talina Valentine, my company has launched a social media site and campaign that will serve several of our clients and allow us to cross-promote and market their goods and services as a one-stop powerhouse.

We're the leaders of who's who in business. No one will touch what we've just created. I smile proudly. I've watched Talina grow over the last four years. She has found her voice and made me millions, going on billions.

It's time for her to receive a promotion. It's actually long overdue, but I've had the perfect position in my mind for Talina. I've just been grooming her for it, while getting rid of the current holder of said position.

I have other positions I'd love to groom her for, the thought runs unbidden through my head. I frown, as her boyfriend walks up beside her. They look like the perfect couple. Not only is Talina gorgeous with her mocha brown skin, but her boyfriend is tall dark and handsome.

He looks like he could be on the cover of a GQ magazine. Dark chocolate skin, a perfectly well-groomed beard, tailored suit, and he's just as tall as I am, maybe six-three to my six-three and a half.

Watching her small frame stand next to him, I know she would fit me perfectly. Although, I'm not quite as handsome. Oh, I'm an honest man.

Most of the women I date, date me because I have money. When I was dirty and broke, none of the women that drop their drawers for me now would have taken a second look at me. Don't get me wrong.

I used to pull my fair share of women, just not the beauty queens I pull now. I'm confident in who I am, it took me awhile to get there, but I am now. At least, when it comes to every woman but Talina.

I can't believe that at thirty-eight, I turn into a blushing mess around her. It is quite amusing and annoying, I must admit. I've tried to steer clear of her as much as possible because of it.

"She's just as beautiful now, as she was ten minutes ago. You can stop staring." A Hispanic accent purrs beside me.

I turn toward my childhood best friend. The one person that believed in me growing up. I wouldn't have built any of this if it weren't for her. Detra has this determination and ambition that's infectious.

Detra is unique in every way possible, from her Puerto Rican father and Jamaican mother to her carefree style of living her life. Detra believes you have to try everything once.

"What are you talking about?" I murmur, taking a sip of the Brandy I've been nursing for the past hour.

Detra nods out towards the crowd below. "Her, your little dove. You can't fool me. I see the way you look at her. She should have been yours by now," Detra says.

"She's involved," I shrug.

Detra holds out a napkin to me. I lift my brow in question. Her full lips curl in the corners. "It's for the drool," she chuckles.

"Humph," I snort and turn back toward my guests below.

"She's the reason you're up here and not down there with your clients and your accomplishments. This is a wonderful night. You should be down there celebrating." Detra sighs.

"I've just been reflecting on a few things, before I join the party." I shrug.

"Things like her. Who is this boyfriend? Does he deserve her?" Detra looks below, narrowing her eyes.

I turn to her sharply and point a finger. "Don't," I order.

"What?" Detra bats her lashes at me innocently.

"I know you and I know what you're thinking. Don't, I'm warning you. Don't interfere in her life," I say firmly.

"I would never," Detra replies.

"Bullshit, and you know it. Besides, look at him and look at me. You would just be wasting your time," I say turning back to look down at Talina.

"I hate it when you do that. You're an amazing man. You're smart, successful, and you're one of the sweetest men I know when you want to be," Detra says, her voice softening with her last words.

"Nowhere in there did you say handsome or sexy," I scoff.

Detra's eyes widen. "You're insane. I shouldn't have to tell you how sexy you are. The shit oozes off of you. Are you sexy in the traditional movie star way? No. You know I'm not going to bullshit you, but you have this thing.

"I can't explain it. Confidence hums off of you and you just…I don't know. You think the women that date you just do it for the money, but I've seen the satisfied looks on their faces," Detra gives me a mischievous smile.

"And yet, you've never been curious enough to have a try." I purse my lips.

Detra sighs and places a hand on her hips. "First of all, you're my best damn friend. I know way too much about you. We would never work. You'd strangle me five seconds into our relationship, fling, or whatever. Then, I'd have to cut your balls off.

"Secondly," her eyes roll over me, her smile grows wider. "I lied that one time. I did see you naked. I'm just not ready for those types of problems. I like the construction of my walls."

I throw my head back and laugh. It is a deep belly laugh. I figured she'd seen more than she let on. Just hearing her say it— only as she can—is hilarious.

"What? You know what I'm talking about," Detra looks down at my crotch pointedly. "But seriously, you are handsome in your own way."

"Sure." I nod and take another sip of my drink.

Detra frowns. "Where is this coming from? I haven't heard you talk like this in so long."

"It's nothing," I wave it off.

"It's her, but why?" Detra muses aloud.

I think over her question for myself. What makes me so insecure when it comes to Talina? *She's the one.* The thought just pops into my head.

My heart has a mind of its own, when she's around. I've wanted to get to know more about Talina since the day I first laid eyes on her. I stammered over my words and botched the entire interview, like I was the one looking for a job.

I had to excuse myself and let Detra handle the remainder of the meeting. I'd thought I was just off that day. I soon learned it was all because of *her*. Every time Talina is near I forget myself. I become the insecure boy I used to be.

"I don't know," I murmur to Detra, not daring to reveal the truth.

Detra glances at me, as if she can see through me. "Um, I see. You keep telling yourself that," Detra huffs. "For now, let's get to your guests. You worked hard for this."

I sigh, "That I have."

"Oh, and another thing. When and if the opportunity arises for you to pursue her, go after it," Detra says firmly.

"Detra, I'm warning you," I growl.

She holds her dainty hand up. "Remember, I work with these women. We talk from time to time. Things get said and passed around. Not everything you see is perfect. Picture perfect, yes, actually perfect, no."

This time I let her words sink in. I may not fully understand them, but I will admit they give me a sliver of hope. Not much, but enough, for now.

CHAPTER ONE

Meeting Drama

Talina

I smile down at my phone, it's a text from Malcolm. It's my birthday. I thought he forgot this morning, but seeing the text gives me hope. I look up at my boss, talking in the front of the room.

As usual my awkward boss is looking anywhere but at me. Nelson Fisher is an interesting man, both brilliant and ambitious. Over the last four years, I've watched him prove to be a great contradiction.

I've watched from the back of a room, as he commanded a meeting. So much confidence and strength. He reeks of power when he is in his element.

Yet, I've seen him fumble over something as simple as my initial interview. It's like watching two different men. I swear, I once thought he had a twin or something. Almost as if they take turns coming to work.

His right hand, Detra has always been there like his saving grace. I once thought they were an item. Rumor has it, they are just very good friends, more like brother and sister.

Detra's nickname around the office is, *the pit bull*. She will chew anyone up and spit them out for Nelson. I've gotten glimpses of his sweet side. I'm glad that he has Detra. I think the wrong person would try to take advantage of that side of Nelson.

That thought makes me smile. I've also seen the man chew a few people up and spit them out for himself. He can be a very shrewd businessman. As I said, a contradiction in every way.

After confirming that Nelson isn't giving me any attention, I try to discretely swipe open the text. I frown and sink lower into my seat, when I read that Malcolm has only sent a text asking me if everything is set for his parents' anniversary party. It feels like a dagger to the heart.

When I first started dating Malcolm, all he talked about was finding the right woman he could settle down with. One to have a family with. He wanted someone educated that he could hold a conversation with, someone he could build with. He claimed to want a financially stable woman.

Here I am. I tick off all of those boxes and some. Yet, we've been dating for five years and I feel like we are growing further apart, rather than together. Hell, I'm afraid to tell him about the bonus check I received last month from the multiple accounts I helped the company acquire with that social media campaign.

"I think we should host a party in LA for the REX account. I was just telling my team that we'll cover more ground that way, in terms of new clients and targeting all of our existing clients' needs," my head snaps up, as I hear my own ideas being passed off word for word.

I look in the direction of our executive director. Art is a grade A, top notch, certified asshole. Sometimes, I don't even think Nelson likes him. I think he has been tolerating him, as if he has just been waiting to replace him with the right person.

Detra has no patience for Art, most times she pretends he's not even in the room. No, seriously, she has been known to ignore his words directed towards her, as if he never said a word.

My eyes focus on Art. He's doing his best not to look at me. I look around the room at the other mix of faces. Some have a look of disgust, others look awed, but not surprised. I just presented this idea in the morning team prep meeting.

He shot it down as a terrible idea. His words were, 'It's too costly…we shouldn't be using an idea of this scale with REX…Nelson will hate that idea.' Yet, here he is, spewing my words like they're his own.

I can feel my blood boiling, as I take another glance around the room, waiting for someone to speak up. I know it's not going to happen, I just can't believe it.

This isn't the first-time Art has done this to someone. It's par for the course around here. Although, it's the first he's tried it with me and I'm not having it.

I sit up in my seat, ready to go to battle for my hard work and ideas. However, there's a face that draws my attention. Nelson is glaring at Art.

Nelson tilts his head, while staring at the man. "Have you looked into making this happen? What are the numbers, what venue were you thinking about?" Nelson responds.

I bite my lip in anger and dip my head. I don't want to be that woman. Nelson is the CEO of the company. I weigh the consequences of airing Art's ass out, in front of our big boss.

I look up through my lashes to see Art shift some papers around in front of him. His ass looks lost, he has no numbers or details on this. It's not his fucking idea. I have all of the information in a file back in my office.

"I handed the mock up and specs to Talina. Talina, can you fill Nelson in?"

"Excuse me," I snap, my head popping up.

I look back to Nelson. It's odd, but he looks as if he wants to commit murder. I'm thrown for a minute, as I look at him and his reaction.

Figuring he's going to ream me for being unprepared, I get ready to open my mouth. Nelson's eyes slide to me, and he gives a slight shake of his head, causing me to clamp my mouth shut.

"Talina, Nelson asked you for the report. Would you be so kind as to focus on your job? You can daydream later, back in that undeserved office," Art snarls at me.

Nelson stands from his seat so swiftly, it flies back. All heads turn to him, but his glare is on Art. My heart is pounding in my chest, my head feels like it's going to explode.

I'm already planning to curse Art's ass out later, in private. This doesn't look like the meeting to call foul in. Fucking creep, he has been an extra asshole the last few weeks, since the holiday party. I've bitten my tongue enough. He's my superior, but I always demand his respect.

"Sir—," I get ready to address Nelson.

He raises his hand in my direction cutting me off. I swallow my words and cut my eyes to Detra. She just gives me a smirk and nods her head slightly for me to be silent.

Detra has always been nice to me. Oddly enough, in the last few weeks, she has been stopping by my office more than usual to ask my opinion on a whole lot.

I didn't think it was odd, until yesterday. Her questions were centered more on Nelson, not really marketing. Or at least, it didn't seem that way.

"I think my ears must have failed me. Did you just speak to *my* employee that way? Especially, when I didn't ask her for anything. I asked you, as it is your department and as you said, *your* idea," Nelson says, with a very deceptive calm.

"Nelson, I—," Art spatters.

"You what? Like trying to embarrass people because of your power and position. How dare you insinuate that Talina hasn't earned her office? She has pulled in millions for this company in this last quarter alone.

"Art, tell me when was the last time you added value to this company? Yes, I'm asking you this in front of everyone. I want you to know how it feels," Nelson says as his voice rumbles.

"I have led the teams that have secured our top clients," Art puffs out his chest.

Nelson snorts. "I think I have displayed signs of being the village idiot. I must have. Do you think I don't watch what goes on in my own company?"

"I don't think that at all," Art tries to back pedal. "I know you are observant over all of our accounts."

"Shut up," Nelson booms.

I look at Nelson through new a lens. Something about the way he is taking charge of this situation is hot. I tilt my head and look at my boss more closely.

Nelson isn't your traditional good-looking man. For one, he has a large nose that dominates his face. It's not just long, but a bit on the wide side. It looks like it may have even been broken a time or two.

Nelson is on the paler side. With the long hours he works, I can't see that changing much. I don't know when this man sees the sun.

Yet, today, I'm looking beyond all of that. His hazel eyes are inviting, and his lips are full in a well-proportioned way. I never noticed before, but he has the longest lashes I've ever seen on a man.

His brown hair is always neatly combed, sometimes even gelled into place, but in this moment it has fallen into his forehead. If he had on his glasses that are usually perched on his nose during meetings, I would think of Clark Kent.

My eyes slide down his body. Well, damn. Why have I never noticed how hot Nelson's body is? The way he's standing now oozes sex appeal.

"Talina," Nelson says my name roughly, pulling my eyes away from his crotch.

I mentally slap myself. *Why the hell am I ogling my boss? I have a boyfriend.*

My eyes snap up to Nelson's face. "Come," he says.

I promise you. I think I do, which startles the fuck out of me. The rawness of his voice rubs me in ways it just shouldn't.

I stand quickly and round the table. When I stand beside Nelson, I look at a red-faced Art. Art's eyes burn into me. If looks could kill, I'd be dead.

Nelson places his hand on the small of my back. I jump a little before catching myself. It isn't that I'm offended by the touch. It is just the opposite.

The electricity that passes between us is enough to make my knees buckle. I'm surprised and unwitted by it. It totally takes me off guard.

Thankfully, Nelson quickly removes his hand. I chide myself at the bereft feeling I have. I look up to see his cheeks have taken on a little color. I don't know if it's from his anger or if he too felt the charge I just did.

"Do you know what I find funny, Art?" Nelson hisses.

"I'm not sure what could be funny about this," Art mumbles just audibly.

"During our holiday party, Talina and I had a few glasses of champagne to celebrate with our clients. What she failed to tell me prior is that while she can consume other alcohols with more tolerance, champagne loosens her lips.

"Talina's date had to leave suddenly, but she remained with myself and the clients. Which, was partly because no one could find you. Talina was gracious in stepping in for you.

"Just so happens, Detra and I ended the night, placing Talina in a cab, after a very interesting evening. One where she talked for hours. During that time, I want you to guess which one of the many ideas she has in her brilliant mind, she happened to share with me." Nelson levels Art with a hard glare.

I'm mortified. I vaguely remember the events he's talking about. I want to curl into a ball and crawl under the conference table.

I can drink Tequila like a champ and be as right as rain. Give me champagne and I will talk you to death. The room starts to spin. I don't know where Nelson is going with this.

Seconds that seem like minutes pass and the floor has yet to open and swallow me up. If I get fired today, I'm keying Art's car and slashing his tires. I'm just in one of those moods.

I was covering for his sorry ass when I had that toast with Nelson and our clients. Malcolm had had an emergency, but he told me to stay behind. That's when Detra came to get me, stating Nelson needed someone from the team. She couldn't find Art.

I groan internally, hoping I didn't embarrass myself in front of my boss or our clients. I had about three glasses, which means, I probably talked too much, was very bossy, and most likely way too chipper.

Nelson's voice brings me back from my inner agony. "Talina, I was going to save this announcement for the New Year. However, I think now is as good a time as any," Nelson says, while looking down at me. He then looks away to the rest of the room.

"Talina single handedly secured us a twenty-million-dollar bonus from one of our top clients. A new project was tossed out by our client's wife, and Talina pitched a full-blown campaign on the spot.

"I've never seen anything like it. Armed with her phone, a pen, and a few napkins to draw out a presentation right before our eyes. The contracts were signed and delivered this morning.

"After watching her in action, Detra and I sat and picked her brain for a few more hours. The REX idea was pitched weeks ago. That's why it wasn't on this morning's revised agenda. We're already in contract.

"I just want to thank you Art for not paying more attention to *your* work," Nelson snorts. "It's now very clear who I have working for me."

"I would never take my team's ideas. I may have heard her mention a few ideas, that sparked my pitch," Art tries.

"Save it," Nelson growls. "Talina will be taking over as the new executive director, she will also be our head US and International analyst and developmental advisor," Nelson announces.

"Excuse me," my head snaps back, my eyes grow wide.

"Congratulations, it has been a long time coming," Nelson says with a smile.

This time my legs do buckle. Nelson is swift to catch me around the waist and guide me to the seat he emptied earlier. He squats before me, handing me the glass of water Detra hands to him.

I can see the actions of everyone. I just can't comprehend anything beyond that. My ears are buzzing. I've dreamed of a promotion like this one. Keyword, *dreamed*.

Art has been with the company for years. Nelson is right, Art is a leach. He doesn't offer any fresh ideas and has been known to claim other peoples' ideas for his own. However, he has held his position for way longer than I've been here.

Nelson has just essentially announced that he's giving me Art's job, plus the position Art had been hoping to acquire as Nelson expands the company. Everyone knows Art has had his eyes set on the US and International advisory position.

It's all our team has heard about in the last few months. We all worked our asses off so Art would get the position. At least, everyone except for Art has worked their ass off for him to get the promotion.

"What?" Art roars, breaking through my haze. "Nelson, what the hell are you talking about?"

Nelson doesn't reply. Instead, he keeps his eyes on mine. "Are you okay?" Nelson murmurs to me.

I can see the concern in his face. I feel my face heat with embarrassment. Everyone's eyes are on me and my boss. I blink a few times, hoping to find my equilibrium.

"Drink some more water," Nelson coaches.

I hadn't realized I took the first sip. I nod my head and take another drink. I drain the glass this time, as my eyes dart around the room.

"Focus on me," Nelson says soothingly.

"Nelson, clearly she's not ready for a promotion like this. Just look. What does this mean for me? I've given you ten years of my life. I started with you when you were a snot nosed kid with nothing," Art snarls.

Nelson spins away from me and lifts to his full height. "I'd stop right there if I were you. You started with me when I had nothing and you've been trying to send me right back to nothing," Nelson snarls.

Just then security enters the room. I turn to see Detra with a smile on her lips. I suddenly get the feeling I've been put in the middle of something so much bigger than me.

"I have been waiting for this day," Detra purrs. "I can't stand a thief or a traitor."

"Wh...what?" Art spatters.

"Like I said. You must of thought I was some type of idiot," Nelson says dryly.

"Nelson, I don't know what you think you know," Art says nervously.

"Shut the fuck up. You've lied and stolen from me enough. I had intended to wait to do this. I wanted to give you the opportunity to explain yourself, but I won't have you here treating my loyal employees like shit under your shoe," Nelson growls.

"Should they detain him?" Detra asks.

"I want him out of my building. My attorneys will be in touch, Art. This I can assure you," Nelson replies.

I almost want to laugh at the way Art flails around while being escorted from the conference room. Actually, a bit of a laugh does bubble up to my lips. I feel like I'm having an out of body experience.

Nelson turns back to me. A curious look in his eyes. He tilts his head and studies me closely.

"Everyone, you're dismissed. We'll schedule a meeting for when I return. By then, things should have settled around here," Nelson announces to the room.

I go to get up, but he gives a slight nod for me to remain seated. He squats before me once again. Reaching over to the table with his long arms, he pours another glass of water.

When he turns towards me, he hands over the glass. I hear the door close as the room empties. I take the water and shift in my seat a bit. I'm so embarrassed.

Here, this man has just handed over the promotion of my dreams and I nearly pass out in front of the entire staff. I feel like a moron. It's just, he caught me off guard. I thought I was going to be called out for being a babbling drunk, during a work function, not given a promotion.

"I shouldn't have lost my temper like that. I'd planned to promote you privately, after my trip to London," Nelson mutters, a blush coming to his cheeks.

"It's…it's okay. I was just surprised," I say softly.

He nods. "Yes, I can see that. I hope you want the job. The advisory position will lead to more travel. Nearly half of next year will be spent setting up the new office with myself and Detra."

"Yes, of course, I definitely want the job. I'm just hoping you still want to give it to me," I bite my lip and groan internally at how my words come out.

Nelson's close proximity is starting to register with my head and my body. I can feel the heat coming off of him. It's the strangest thing, but I feel this pull towards him that I've never felt before.

Nelson is so not my usual type, but I'd be lying to say I don't feel a serious attraction toward him in this moment. I've never given him much attention, but up this close, there is something appealing about him. Not like Malcolm, who can wink and your panties would melt off.

No, I can't put my finger on it, but there is something attractive about Nelson. Oh, and the blush on his cheeks is darn right adorable. His eyes search mine.

"I've been wanting to give it to you for a long time," he says.

My eyes close as my pussy pulses between my legs. I think I've lost my mind. Still, that soft rasp to his voice. The one I've never given notice to before, is hot as hell.

"Um, I think I should get back to my office. I can pinch myself in there and do a little squeal if this all turns out to be real." I give a soft laugh.

Nelson gives a small chuckle and stands. "It's real. Again, I do apologize for how I've handled this," he says, and takes a step back to give me room.

"No worries." I shrug and stand.

I sway a little at first, causing my face to burn a little more. I take a breath and pull my shit together. I've worked my ass off for this promotion. I deserve it.

Get it together, Talina. You rocked that social media campaign. And bagged a twenty-million-dollar account, while drunk off champagne. Boss! You earned this.

I move quickly to make my exit, before Nelson can take back my new promotion, due to my sudden lack of sense. However, his voice washes over me, stopping me at the door. I pause with my hand on the knob.

~B~

Nelson

I know I should just let her walk out of that door. I've already skirted such a fine line. Being so close to her, I've had to call on all of my restraint. In reality, I want nothing more than to take her sexy brown body right here on the conference table.

I should've kept my mouth shut, but watching her ass sway, as she moved to leave the room, has fried my brain and common sense along with it. No, to be truthful, I lost my common sense the moment Art decided to steal Talina's idea and talk to her like shit. I'd planned to have his ass thrown in a handbasket, I just wanted to get a few more ducks in a row.

Unfortunately, for him, I will never stand for anyone talking to Talina that way. Whether she's mine or not. It will never happen in my presence.

"Talina," I call, stopping her in her tracks.

I hadn't planned on taking her on the trip to London with me, but I want her there now. No, I need her there. I look away, when her big, oval brown eyes connect with mine, instantly cursing myself for the move.

"Yes," she replies.

"Now that I've announced the promotion. I would like you to accompany me to London. It will be a great way for you to get caught up and meet the team there. I hope that isn't a problem. I know it's last minute," I say.

"Oh," her eyes round. I can see the wheels turning in her pretty head, as I look up through my lashes at her. She bites down on that full lip. "Well, I have my boyfriend's parents' anniversary party next week. They would totally understand and I would be willing to go, but I sort of organized the entire thing.

"I'll have to see if someone can take over for me. Malcolm hasn't been too involved. I'd need to get him up to speed," she rambles on, trying to make it work in her head. Those long lashes blinking, as her mind turns.

"No, no," I interrupt her. "I will move things around. I don't leave until Friday, but you can come in after, if that's okay."

"Are you sure, I think I can make it work," she gives me that bright smile of hers. The one that makes her full cheeks rise and brightens her mocha face.

"I will not ruin your plans. This was short notice. Please, I'll have Detra arrange for you to join me after," I nod and give a tight smile.

"Thank you so much. I don't think I've said thank you," Talina says, sounding more like herself.

"You're welcome. It's well deserved," I reply. "Talina."

"Yes, Sir," she says, with that infectious smile.

"Happy birthday," I reply.

Her brown eyes grow again, and her cheeks light up with a glow. "Thank you," she says, her brows wrinkling a little after saying the words.

My cell phone rings, breaking the exchange, before I can embarrass myself anymore today. I nod at Talina and take the call. She slips out of the room and I can think straight for the first time since Art opened his mouth to steal from her.

I shouldn't have invited her on this trip. She is involved and I just gave her a huge promotion. I would hate for her to think it was done because I'm trying to sleep with her.

Talina earned this promotion. I sigh. I'll have to ask Detra to come along as well to keep my head on straight. The last thing I need is a sexual harassment case. Not that I would try to force myself on Talina.

What is it about her? What the hell are you doing?

I honestly have no idea.

CHAPTER TWO

He Likes You

Talina

I rush into the ladies' room to splash some water on my face. This is so unreal. My head is still spinning from it all. I know I could've handled that more professionally. It's been years since I had a panic attack.

Turning on the faucet and wetting a napkin, I begin to dab my face. While looking at my reflection it hits me. I just got a promotion. I will be making twice my salary.

I'm going to London!

I start to jump around and do a happy dance. I nearly jump out of my skin, as the bathroom door flies open. My friend, Marsha, bursts into the bathroom with a beaming smile on her face. We dance and jump around together, squealing low enough for just us to hear.

"That was so fucking awesome," Marsha squeals, with a hint of her West Indian accent. "I've never seen Nelson lose his shit like that before. I mean, I've seen him go off a time or two, but nothing like that."

"Oh, my God. I know, right. I thought he was going to light into my ass too. Not give me a promotion," I say in disbelief.

"Honey," Marsha fans her face. "I've always thought he had a thing for you, but that right there, it totally proved me right."

I frown and knit my brows. "What are you talking about?"

Marsha side glances me. Her lips twist and her hands go to her hips. She's giving me a her *'you've got to be fucking kidding me'* look.

"Gal, you are a small wonder sometimes. These men be out here falling all over your ass and you haven't got the slightest clue. You seriously have never noticed the way Nelson looks or acts 'round you?" Marsha says.

"No," I reply, knitting my brows further.

"Lawrt, gal, I don't know what's worse. The fact that you don't know you're a catch. Or the fact that you don't see that you're in a dead relationship," Marsha sighs.

My shoulders sag. "Please don't start in on that," I huff.

"So, what he get you for your birthday?" Marsha pushes.

"Not going there," I huff.

"Umm," Marsha murmurs. "All I'm saying is, you're gorgeous, smart, and just received an awesome promotion. When are you going to stop letting that man string you along?"

I open my mouth to reply, but I have nothing to say. She's right. I've come to realize that in the last few weeks. I just don't know what to do. I think I've become comfortable.

I shrug my shoulders instead. I don't want to come down from the high of my promotion. It was just setting in. However, I know I need to get my personal life in order.

"Hey, I'm sorry," Marsha says, when she notices me drawing into myself. "Let me make it up to you. Drinks after work, on me."

I press my lips and think about it. Malcolm clearly forgot what today is. Why shouldn't I celebrate my promotion and my birthday? I shrug my shoulders and give her a smile.

"Okay, just a couple." I nod.

"That's my girl," Marsha purrs.

~B~

Detra

Nelson is like a brother to me. I know when he wants something, even when he refuses to admit it to himself. He wants Talina Valentine.

I step out of the bathroom stall and look at the door, she and Marsha Evans just walked through. I know an unhappy relationship when I see one. I don't much care for Talina's boyfriend, Malcolm.

He's a decent guy, I just don't like them as a couple. They're beautiful to look at together, but I always get the impression he wants to be somewhere else.

I know Nelson told me to mind my business. I just can't sit back and watch this any longer. After watching those two in that meeting today, I think Nelson may be underestimating himself.

The chemistry between them is undeniable. It was pouring off of them in droves. Anyone could see the attraction that's no longer one sided.

A week ago, I may have told Nelson to move on. However, not after watching those two today. Talina has finally noticed Nelson, whether she's ready to admit it or not.

Since high school, Nelson has this thing with girls he really likes. He clams up and starts that insecure bullshit. It's his mom's fault if you ask me.

Nelson had a shitty childhood and that woman did nothing to make it better. Always calling him names and telling him he would be nothing. If Nelson questions his looks, it's because of her. That woman is sheer evil.

I tap my chin, squinting at the closed bathroom door. With my mind made up, I pull my phone out. This is what Nelson keeps me around for. I'm the watcher, the fixer, the muscle, and the advisor. It's time I do my job concerning his love life.

"Hello," I say into my phone with a smile.

"What's this call going to cost me this time," the voice on the other end says.

"I'm the one in need of a favor this time, brother," I smile into the phone.

"Thank goodness," the voice sighs teasingly on the other end. "I have a drop of blood left, I know you're coming for it one of these days."

"Just not today, poppy," I chuckle.

"I want you to look into someone for me," I start to instruct.

I know Nelson is going to be pissed. I just want to get all of the facts, before I start to meddle. *No harm, no foul.*

CHAPTER THREE

It's Over

Talina

I can say without a doubt that my best friend, Marsha Evans, ain't shit. We were supposed to go for a few drinks. Nothing to get me shit faced and stumbling. It's only Tuesday, for Christ's sake.

Well, actually, it's now Wednesday morning, as I tip toe into my apartment. I'm so roasted, I just spent thirty minutes across the hall trying to get into my neighbor's apartment. Lord, help me. I need to be at work in a few hours.

I haven't had so much fun in years. I think I laughed the hardest I ever have in my life. I smile, leaning my back against the door, thinking of Marsha's antics. I shake my head, my smile still consuming my face.

At thirty-three, I don't think we're old enough to be cougars, but she robbed the cradle tonight. Don't get me wrong, he was cute, just a bit on the young side. No more than twenty-four, if you ask me.

"If I came in this house at this time of night, you would have a fit," Malcolm's voice booms through the room, startling me, as he flicks on the lights.

My smile slips from my lips and my shoulders sag. I was hoping to avoid this. After calling Malcolm with the news of my new promotion and his less than stellar response, I needed a night out with my girl.

Mind you, he has yet to acknowledge my birthday. When I asked if he would be okay with me going out for a drink after work, he brushed it off, as if it was nothing. I spent the first half of my night wondering why I'm even in this relationship.

"Malcolm, it's late. I just want a shower and to go to bed," I sigh.

"I think we need to talk," Malcolm says, folding his arms over his chest.

I huff, bending to place my shoes on the floor beside me. I place my bags on the table by the door and move forward towards the bedroom. Malcolm keeps his chocolate gaze on me.

"About what?" I mumble.

"We need to talk about us," he replies.

"Okay, what about us?" I ask, getting annoyed.

"About the fact that I don't think this is working." Malcolm shrugs.

I stop in my tracks and look up at the man I've been building a life with for the last five years. My sister warned me about Malcolm moving in with me. She's never been a fan of our relationship.

It's not so much Malcolm, it's us as a couple. Myra has never felt Malcolm and I fit. My sister is also seeing an Asian man, which Malcolm has issues with. So, I've tried to separate Myra's feelings from my own.

Malcolm has a lot of strong opinions that I can never say are my own. I've just silently agreed to disagree. Yet, never has he expressed that this relationship hasn't been working for him.

"Excuse me?" I slur a bit, although, I'm sobering real fast.

"Ta, we're going in two different directions." Malcolm sighs and rubs his forehead.

"Okay," I nod and place my hands on my hips.

"Listen, you're a great girl. My family loves you, you have a good head on your shoulders. You're beautiful," he continues, but I have to stop him.

"First of all, at thirty-three, I'm not a girl," I correct him. "Your family would love me, I treat them like my own. Malcolm, help me understand this. How long have you known you were unhappy in this relationship with me?"

"Baby," he starts, but I hold my hand up and shake my head.

"You can save that baby BS for the next," I sass.

"Ta, things were good in the beginning. I really thought you were the one. It's just," he pauses and purses his lips.

I sigh, and lower to the floor so the room will stop spinning. I cross my legs and look up at the man I've treated like a king for the past five years. He is still gorgeous, a breathtaking black man.

Malcolm is smart, he can be driven when he wants to be, he's sexy as fuck, and Lord, does he know how to take my body there. My brows wrinkle. I just can't remember the last time he tried to take my body there. I know I've been working later and longer hours the last few months.

I guess I didn't have time to notice it all falling apart. Yeah, Marsha has pried a number of times. I just don't share my business like that. The little she does know happens to be from being around us.

"Are you cheating on me?" I ask, as my thoughts race.

Malcolm sighs and lowers to sit in front of me. He lifts my chin with his fingertips, looking me in my eyes. Those soulful brown orbs of his were one of the first things I fell in love with.

"You and I both know that's not me. Yes, I'm interested in someone, I'm not going to lie about that. I just haven't pursued anything. I have too much respect for you and the time you've given me," he replies.

I snort and pull my face away. "Respect for my time would have been breaking this off, four and a half years ago," I mutter.

"Ta, four and a half years ago, you had me so sprung, I was ready to marry you then," Malcolm says.

"Then, what happened? Did I grow a second head?" I snap.

"You grew a career," Malcolm murmurs. "Don't get me wrong. I'm so fucking proud of you. Today, when you called about your promotion, I wanted to jump on my desk and shout for you.

"Then, it dawned on me. You've been talking about that promotion and how it meant your supervisor would have to travel more. If you're now your supervisor, and you're taking his promotion, then, you'll be the one traveling," Malcolm rubs his forehead.

I knit my brows. "Malcolm, I asked you when we met would my career be a problem for you. You told me, no. You said you respected my goals and ambitions. You said you wanted a woman to build with," I can hear the frustration in my own voice.

"Yeah, I know. I just didn't think you were going after such a high corporate ladder," he shrugs.

"Are you fucking serious?"

"Damn, Ta, I know this shit sounds fucked up," Malcolm groans. "But do you have any idea how it feels when my father asks me when I'm going to grow up and make moves like you? When I'm going to buy you a place and stop living off of you?"

"Malcolm, you don't live off of me. Your job is great," I interject.

"Baby," he pauses and sighs. "Ta, you make the upper end of six figures. This new promotion is tipping you over into another tax bracket my black ass will never see at my job. We talked about starting a business, but with the track you're on, I don't see that happening."

"Malcolm, every time I've mentioned sitting down to start the business plan, you shift gears or come up with some excuse why we should wait," I say incredulously. "I have the money squared away for the business."

"Exactly, you have the money squared away. Not we," Malcolm raises his voice. "I started this year with a plan. Put up money for the business and to buy your engagement ring. When I actually went to save the money, it dawned on me how much you take care of around here.

"I started to see how much I lost myself in this place of…comfort. Yeah, that's it. I got too comfortable with having a great woman taking care of so much for me. Just look at the party you're throwing my parents. That shit has blown my mind, Ta. You went all out for them.

"I've been so embarrassed that I've just become complacent, but I don't know what to do. I don't know how to fix this shit. I love you. God, do I love you, but I don't think I'm right for you," Malcolm says, looking away.

I'm floored. A part of me wants to be pissed, it wants to go off and tell him where he can take all of that shit, but there is a part of me that totally understands. I understand because I know this man. He has been my best friend for five years.

"Damn, Malcolm, why not come to me sooner? Why not tell me this so we could work through it? Do you think I don't love you? You're bringing this to me now, when you're already ready to walk out of the door," I shake my head. "That's some fucked up shit, I don't deserve that either, Mal."

"Yeah, I know. It just hit home today. I was trying to figure out how to say something, then today...I'm sorry," he finishes.

"So, it has nothing to do with this woman you're interested in," I purse my lips.

I'm not going to act like I didn't catch that one. Malcolm looks at me, I can see him thinking. Probably trying to figure out how to say this without getting the taste slapped out of his mouth.

"When I first noticed her, I noticed everything about her that isn't you. I think that's the crazy part. I know what I have. I know I'm a fool for letting go of what I have, but nah, it's not because of her," he finally says.

"I think I need to be alone for a while. You know, figure out where I'm going. What's my next step?" He nods at his own words.

My head whips back. There's no need for us to further this discussion. He is already gone. I blink back the tears I was going to shed.

My mom raised me to know my value. I'm not about to sit on this floor and beg this man to love me. No, that's what we're not gonna do.

"I'm going to bed, Malcolm. You handle your business. But you remember this, I bet you'll start loving me as soon as I start loving someone else. I guarantee it. You just remember, you had your chance.

"You made the choice to go from being someone's King to another woman's maybe. You know me and you knew, from day one, I never look back. I wish you happiness, Mal, but you just gave up bliss," I finish, get to my feet and enter my bedroom.

My heart aches, as I close the door on a chapter of my life. I'm too numb to know how I feel.

Happy fucking Birthday.

CHAPTER FOUR

Lunch

Talina

My head is pounding. I should've just called in today. I almost did, but I didn't think it was a good idea after just getting a big promotion. I would hate for Nelson to feel he made a mistake.

I groan when a knock sounds on my office door. I look up to see Marsha standing there with sunglasses on. She gives me a little smirk.

Evil wench.

"Enough packing this office up. Let's go get some lunch," she says.

"Can I get a bed with that?" I mutter, and drop my head to my desk.

"Girl, you are usually the recovery champ. Don't tell me last night got the best of you," she laughs.

"Must you be so loud," I huff.

Marsha laughs some more. "I'm damn near whispering," she giggles.

"Ugh, I hate my life," I groan.

"Girl, you just got a bomb ass promotion. A little hangover isn't enough to be talking that mess," Marsha grumbles, pushing the door closed behind her, walking into my office, and sitting in front of my desk.

"Malcolm and I broke up last night," I mutter.

"Thank you, Jesus," she exclaims. "Oh, wait, that was wrong. I mean, hey girl, it's going to be okay. I'm so sad to see him go."

I lift my head slightly and give her the stink eye. That smile on her face has me wanting to slap her. I still haven't decided how I fully feel about what happened last night.

"You know you can get your ass out of my office," I snap, placing my head back down on the desk.

"Okay, okay, I'm sorry. I do know that you loved him, but can I be honest?" Marsha says sincerely.

"You're going to be you. Spit it out," I groan and sit up.

"You and Malcolm are amazing as friends. You truly are. I just think you two were looking for something different from go. You were a trophy on his arm and he was the epitome of what they tell us the perfect man should look like," she shrugs. "However, when you took a deeper look, you two were homies. Not a couple."

"You sound like my sister. What ever happened to friends first? I thought that if you built a friendship first, you're supposed to have a good foundation," I huff.

"Yeah, but some friendships are meant to stay in the friend zone," Marsha shrugs.

"Mm, let's get out of here. I'll tell you what went down last night. I need to know if I've just become heartless.

"Honestly, I'm sort of over it. I mean, I'm hurt, but the things he said. I think I'm just going to throw in the towel," I blow out a breath and retrieve my purse.

"Throwing in the towel?" Marsha kisses her teeth. "Gal, I'm starving. I burned off a lot of energy last night," she winks and stands. "You need to try you a youngin'."

"If you don't get your nasty butt out of my office," I laugh, walking to the door. "Honestly, I don't think relationships are for me. I think I'm done with men."

"Whatever," Marsha sucks her teeth again.

"I'm serious," I look back to say.

I run right into a hard body and almost stumble back. Strong arms wrap my waist, preventing me from hitting the floor. I turn to look up, as the arms tighten to draw me nearer and steady me.

"Oh, I'm so sorry, Nelson."

I just can't catch a break this week. I've embarrassed myself in front of this man more times than I can count.

He doesn't reply right away, or release me for that matter. Although, there's a strange look in his eyes, when I look up into them. I move to step out of his hold, not liking how bereaved I feel when his arms fall away.

"It was my fault," he clears his throat and says. "I was on my way to your office. I wasn't looking where I was going."

"Did you need something? We were just about to step out for lunch," I say.

"Can I join you?" His cheeks pink. "I meant, can I buy you lunch for almost trampling you?"

I open my mouth, but I don't know what to say. I had planned to dish with my girl. I wasn't planning on sitting through a business lunch.

"I promise, I won't talk shop. There's this great Thai place not far from here. Is Thai still one of your favorites?" he says, in the wake of my absence of words.

"Yes," I say knitting my brows.

"Your first year here, I kept you late a few times. You were craving Thai one evening," Nelson starts by way of explanation.

"Oh, yeah, and you had someone find a Thai place that was open so late. I remember that. I can't believe you remembered," I say in astonishment. It reminds me of the fact that he remembered my birthday yesterday.

"Mr. Fisher, we would love to have lunch with you," Marsha interrupts.

"Nelson, you know I'm never that formal, Marsha," Nelson replies.

I turn to glare at her. *What?* I mouth. She waves me off and keeps talking. I swear, I want to kill her.

"I think Ta could use some Thai food to cheer her up," Marsha chirps.

"Oh really, what has you down? I hope it's not the promotion. If you want to discuss your salary, it's negotiable. You're a valued asset here. I'd be more than willing to increase the offer," Nelson says, looking down at me.

My mouth flaps open. Why have I become a mute around this man? I can't seem to string a sentence together in front of him in the last few days.

"No, no, it's not the job. She and her boyfriend broke up," Marsha says.

"Marsha," I find my voice and hiss.

"Oh, I'm sorry to hear that. In that case, we're all taking the rest of the day off," Nelson says with a beaming smile.

"Huh?" I look up at him.

"Whenever Detra has a bad break up, we take the day off," Nelson leans in to whisper.

His cologne floats up my nostrils, making me want to inhale so deeply, I barely refrain from doing so. He smells so good. I can't believe I never noticed before.

"We go out to eat and we shop," he winks at me. "I can't tell you how much retail therapy I've done over the years. I'm a pro."

I narrow my eyes up at him. "Is this some type of test?"

Nelson laughs. "No, it's not. Come on, there's always tomorrow. You work too hard anyway," Nelson says with a crooked smile.

I find it an endearing smile. It brightens his face. His hand falls to the small of my back, as he leads me forward. I turn to look at Marsha, but she's not walking with us. Instead, she is fumbling in her purse.

"Wait, Marsha, are you coming?" I call behind me.

"Um, uh, I can't find my wallet. Maybe next time," she replies and darts in the direction of her office before I can get another word out.

"Heifer," I mutter under my breath.

"I could call Detra to come along if you like," Nelson says beside me.

When I look up to find his eyes, I see disappointment in them. My curiosity is piqued. Nelson has always been on the up and up with me. I've never been uncomfortable around him.

I shrug my shoulders. "A day off to go shopping, or staying at my desk?" I smile up at him. "Come on, Boss. You've figured out one of my guilty pleasures."

I watch the light come back into his eyes. "Great."

~B~

Nelson

I'd been on my way to set up a meeting with Talina when I overheard her say she was done with men. I wasn't trying to eavesdrop. Hearing her words stopped me in my tracks and sent my thoughts flying.

I didn't have time to move away from her office, before she ran right into my chest. I can't get how good she felt in my arms out of my head. She fits me to a Tee, just like I've always thought she would.

When Marsha confirmed that Talina broke things off with her boyfriend, I had to find out more. My foot was in my mouth before I could stop myself and I don't regret it one bit. I haven't had this much fun with a woman, outside of Detra, in years. Not even with Detra.

"Oh, my God, you're hilarious," Talina giggles, as we walk out of another shop, loaded down with bags.

"Come on, you can't tell me you weren't thinking the same thing," I pull a face.

Talina bites her lip and nods her head, holding back a laugh. "She was seriously loud," she bursts into laughter. Talina is referring to another customer in the shop that had been talking on her phone. "I can't believe you said that to her."

"What? I was being honest. No one wanted to hear about her Botox or the hot yoga instructor," I shrug.

"I don't know what was funnier. That you interrupted her to tell her as much, or that you said it with a straight face," Talina says through her laughter.

"I think I was rather polite about it." I mock frown. I hand the bags over to my driver so we can move on to the next shop.

Talina wraps her arms around my bicep. "This has been just what I needed. Thank you so much, Nelson," she says, looking up at me with that gorgeous smile on her lips.

"I'm happy I could be of service. It's not every day I get to spend so much time in such good company," I smile back down at her.

"Ha, you spend your time with models and actresses," she gives me a cheeky smile.

"Yes, but good company is very hard to come by," I shrug. I narrow my eyes. "So, does that mean you keep tabs on my personal life?"

Talina tries to bite back her smile. "You're my boss. It's not keeping tabs," she rolls her eyes and nudges my ribs.

"Um," I say and nudge her back. "What else do you know about me then?"

"You were born and raised in Jersey. You're an only child, you're now rumored to be worth a few million," she winks at me, her comment being modest to say the least. "You give to a lot of charities, but the literacy program is the one nearest to your heart. Why is that?"

I lock eyes with her and search them. I contemplate whether to answer, deciding I want to be honest and share with this beautiful woman on my arm. I take a deep breath and look forward, as we stroll up the street.

"When I was a boy I had this terrible stutter and I couldn't read for shit. I made it all the way to the third grade without anyone catching on. That was when I met Detra," I smile at the memory.

"I used to see her in the neighborhood, but we were in the same class that year. She was the one that picked up on the fact that I couldn't read. I was so good at hiding it. Cheating off of other kids, acting out when asked to read aloud." I frown, as I think of all the trouble I used to get in.

"Detra has the greatest family in the world. They didn't have much, but her parents believed in dreaming big and supporting each other to make those dreams happen. Detra dragged me home with her every day." I begin to smile again.

"Her mother and sisters started to help with my reading. I went from being a shit student to the head of my class. All I needed was the support. I wasn't getting it at home.

"There are so many children that are like I was. No one at home to care. No one to help with their homework, or to get them to read. I was lucky to have the Melendez family. There are children out there that don't have that luxury," I look back at Talina's face to see her reaction.

The warmth I find in her eyes does something to my chest. I've never told anyone that story before. I'm surprised that I've opened up to tell Talina. It has always been a sore point for me.

"Wow, and look at you now," she says, as if she is in awe.

"What about you? What was your family life like?" I ask to get the subject off of me.

I watch as the light dims from her eyes. The smile falls from her lips. I can see the sadness that fills her. I brace myself, hoping she didn't have a rough childhood like I had.

"My parents were great," she says, after a few beats. "I couldn't have asked for a better mom and dad. My sister and I were so lucky to have them.

"My mom was a stay at home mom. We came home to fresh baked cookies and new books all the time. My mother was big on my older sister teaching me what she learned that day in school," she gives a small laugh.

"My dad would come home from work in the evenings and he'd ask us all about our day. Daddy was a civil engineer. He never spoke to us like children. We were just two young adults in his home.

"I still remember the conversation I had with my dad that last night. It was my first year in my own place. I hadn't wanted to go away to school and I hadn't wanted to move out so soon, but Daddy talked me into all of it.

"Living in dorms for my entire college experience. Moving into my first apartment, after grad school. He said, *'It's for the experience, Ta.'* If I'd had stayed home like I wanted...I might have been able to save them. Or I could be dead too." She falls silent.

I'm speechless. I can feel her pain through her words. While I'm grateful she wasn't there, I hurt for her loss.

I wouldn't know what it was like to have that kind of love from my parents, only to have it snatched away. I feel an ache in my chest for her. I don't know what to say. I want to pull her into my arms, I just don't want to overstep my bounds and ruin the time we've spent together.

"We talked about life that night. About living to my fullest potential and being happy. Daddy told me he wanted me to remember to enjoy life," she swipes at a tear. "He shared a quote with me that he read somewhere or something. I can't remember who it was by. I just remember most of the words so clearly.

"It was something like …'live life fully or live life small. Living fully takes courage and is a choice.' Yeah, it was something like that."

"Valorie Burton," I say.

"Huh?" She blinks up at me.

"You're pretty close and it's from a book, by Valorie Burton," I reply.

"Oh, yeah, now I remember. He said that mom was reading something and she shared it with him," she smiles. "Told you mom had a thing for books.

"Wow, I totally forgot to listen to that advice. Later that night, there was a fire. Mom and Dad never made it out," she whispers.

"Oh, God, I'm so sorry," I reply, this time drawing her into a hug.

Talina's arms wrap my waist. We stand in the middle of the busy street for a few moments. Me, giving her my strength and her taking what she needs. It feels so right. I hate to be the one to break the moment, so I don't.

Talina is the first to pull away. "I'm sorry," she sniffles.

"Don't be," I give her a crooked smile. "How about some ice cream?"

Talina gives a small chuckle. "You've fed me and allowed me to torture you with shopping. You have gone above and beyond. I think I should head home. I'm sure Malcolm will need to pack his things." She shrugs. "I know we're parting as friends. At least, I think we are, but I sort of want to make sure he doesn't pull any petty shit."

I frown. "Do you want me to stop by?" I offer.

"Nelson, don't you have a pretty girl to go home to?" she says, with a soft smile.

"No. I'd prefer to wait for a beautiful woman I can go home to one day," I reply.

"She'll be very lucky," Talina says, lifting up on her toes to kiss my cheek. "Thank you for everything, Nelson. This really was a great day and just what I needed."

"At least, let me take you and your things home. There's no way you can get all of that home on the subway," I offer.

She thinks it over for a moment. "Okay, thanks," she answers, turning for the car.

The ride to Talina's home is quiet. She's so lost in her thoughts, I don't think she notices me watching her. She's so beautiful. I wish I knew what her ex was thinking when he let her go.

As if having a sudden thought, Talina turns to me just as we turn the corner into her block. "I think I can leave with you for London on Friday. I won't be attending the anniversary party," she says excitedly.

"Oh, great. I'll stop by your office tomorrow and we can go over a few things. I'll get you up to speed on the trip," I nod.

"Thank you again, Nelson. You really didn't have to do this," she beams at me.

"It was my pleasure. See you tomorrow," I say, with a smile on my lips.

"You got it, Boss," she chirps.

I step out of the car to help her with her bags. Only, as I step from the car, her ex comes out of the building. He moves to Talina's side as she starts to retrieve her bags from my driver. From the glare he gives, I can see I'm not welcomed. Instead of starting a pissing match, I allow him to help Talina with her things.

She turns with an adorable smile on her face, trying to wave goodbye with all of her bags in her hands. Her ex places a possessive hand on her back, leading her inside, carrying the bulk of her bags.

I frown back at him, as he glares me down. Just as I thought, he knows he's giving up a great woman. I can't help but wonder what really happened between them and if it's truly over.

She's going with you to London now. He lost his chance. It's time you make her yours.

CHAPTER FIVE

Second Thoughts

Talina

I haven't stopped smiling since I got home. I'm not even bothered by Malcolm's presence. In fact, I invited him to have dinner with me. I already had plans to whip something up.

I have a stir-fry in the wok in no time. I have a glass of wine in my hand, my favorite tunes on the radio, and a good mood—I haven't had in a long time—fills my apartment. I want to say that it's all the shoes I bought that have me beaming. I just don't think that's entirely true.

Nelson was better company than I thought he would be. Instead of the usual funk I end up in when I talk about my parents, I felt a sort of cleansing after talking to Nelson. I find him so easy to talk to.

I didn't know my boss had such a sense of humor. After lunch, he seemed to relax a lot more. I could see the confident

CEO I've come to know from board meetings and presentations.

"You seem to be in a great mood," Malcolm says, as he walks up behind me.

I look over my shoulder and shrug. My smile slips from my face as I see the look of desire in Malcolm's eyes. I hate that my body instantly responds. It's been so long, but that ship has sailed.

I'm not about to be some booty call for when he's feeling lonely. If we're through, we're through. I shake off my body's reaction as his brown eyes study me.

"Why shouldn't I be?" I lift my shoulder. "I just turned thirty-three and received the promotion of a lifetime. I'll be taking a trip to London, I closed some major accounts, which could open up even more doors," I list, but Malcolm's face sags and his eyes close.

"I can't believe I forgot what yesterday was," he groans low. "Baby, I'm so sorry. I had something planned for months. I had to change things around at the last minute because of work and—," I hold my hand up and shake my head.

"No worries, we're good," I say, and honestly, I mean it.

"You have to let me make it up to you," Malcolm says, cupping my waist and drawing me into him.

I clasp his wrists and pry him off of me. "There's no need. Are you almost done?" I look pointedly at the boxes he has packed.

Malcolm clears his throat. "Yeah, I'll be finished soon," he nods.

"Well, take a break for now. Dinner is ready. I want to eat. I have some work to catch up on," I say, turning to serve our plates.

Malcolm pulls my chair, as I place the two plates down on the table. I take a seat, noting that the air has shifted a bit. I've already let my body know that this man is not ours anymore. She'll have to ignore his presence from here on out.

We eat in silence for a bit, but I feel his eyes on me. I don't want to kill the good vibe I have, so I continue to tap my foot to the music floating through the air while tucking into my food. I close my eyes and sway to Tamar Braxton's, *Love and War*.

"So, London?" Malcolm nods and gives me one of those smiles I used to find breathtaking.

I'm surprised when I don't feel that usual lurch in my chest. I do get excited about my upcoming trip.

"I have so much planning to do. I need to pack, find a house sitter, there's so much to get done before Friday," I say excitedly.

Malcolm drops his fork and makes a sour face. "Friday, when are you returning?"

"I should be back sometime next month or the month after. After the New Year," I reply.

"What the hell, Talina? My parents' party is next week. What about the party? What am I supposed to tell them?" Malcolm growls.

I sit back in my chair and just stare. The food in my mouth sours. I twist my lips, counting backwards in my head. With a sigh, I'm calm enough to reply.

"Let me explain something to you. I planned that party as your girlfriend. We broke up. Your choice. While I won't just let the party fall apart, I'm not obligated to be there and I wouldn't even feel comfortable there at this juncture," I say, as coolly as I can.

"Maybe…I said some things out of anger last night," Malcolm starts.

"I know you, Mal. You spoke your truth last night. Answer me this, have any of your feelings changed from last night?" I ask, watching him closely.

"Yeah, I had time to think."

I lift my hand cutting him off.

"Don't, don't be that guy. You were clear about your feelings. Find yourself, find what you want. I'll have the party planner call you tomorrow," I say and stand.

I take my plate and dump the rest of my food in the trash. I go to tug on a pair of joggers and snatch up my keys. The last twenty-four hours are about to crash down on me. I feel it. I need to get out of this apartment.

I stop at the door, not turning to face Malcolm. I left him sitting at the table, staring into his plate. "Please be gone when I get back," I say softly, I don't wait for his reply.

CHAPTER SIX

Private Meeting

Talina

Once again, I should have called in. My head is pounding as if I have another hang over. As reality set in, a ton of emotions overwhelmed me.

At thirty-three, I thought I would have what my parents had. I've watched friends from college marry and start families. It is a stinging thought that I've yet to find that.

Five years ago, I thought I'd found that in Malcolm. His mother has practically planned our wedding. At most functions, she introduced me as her soon to be daughter-in-law.

I think the shock of the break up wore off when Malcolm tried to turn the tables again. No, that's just not fair to me. Five years, I invested so much into that relationship.

I slam my tablet down on my new desk. I haven't unpacked in my new office, I needed to get some work done first. Only, my brain won't let me focus on a damn thing.

"I can come back at another time," I hear a rich rasp.

I look up to see Nelson's gaze on me. He's leaning into the doorjamb of my new office. His navy suit fitting him like a glove. His black silk tie, and stark white shirt, adding to the frame of the finely made suit.

The smile on his full lips brightens his face, taking away from the harsh planes. I smirk, as I take in his bushy brows and long nose. I wonder if and how he truly broke it in the past.

"No, you're fine," I say with a genuine smile. "How can I help you?"

"I wanted to pop in and talk over the details for London. Detra was supposed to pop in with me," Nelson pauses to frown, seemingly at his own thoughts. "Something came up, but I wanted to at least confirm with you and get you up to speed. We'll be gone for a long time and its already Thursday."

"Sure, sure," I nod. "Detra did email me the itinerary and some notes. I planned to look at them in a few. I have a few projects I want to clean up before we head out."

Nelson moves into the office. It's the first time I take notice of the tablet he's holding in his long fingers. I find that interesting. He always has a tablet attached to him. Normally, that would be the first thing I notice about Nelson, not his suit and looks.

Certainly not the way his large body folds onto the couch in my office. I lift from my desk chair smoothing out the nonexistent wrinkles in my grey sheath dress. It dawns on me how long it took me to get dressed this morning.

I hadn't realized the effort I placed in choosing my outfit or doing my hair until this moment. The red heels were a last minute decision to help me feel like I'm taking some of my power back. Yet, everything else, had been an unconscious decision, even my makeup.

I take a seat on the couch, placing a good enough distance between us for me to not be too close, but to be able to share our devices if necessary. His cologne engulfs me right away. It draws me in like a shoe sale. I lean towards him, crossing my legs.

"I told you that dress would look good on you," Nelson says with a tight smile on his lips.

I look down at my dress and the conversation from yesterday hits me. I hadn't even noticed I picked one of the many things I bought while we shopped together. I smile, looking back up at him.

"You have good taste, Boss. You're a great shopping partner as well," I laugh.

Something crosses Nelson's eyes, but he quickly shuts it down. I want to say I saw disappointment, maybe regret, but I can't put my finger on it for sure. I brush it off and continue to give him an open smile.

"I'm at your service anytime," he says with a small grin. "It is my hope that you will become a part of the team Detra and I have created. We are sort of a family unit, within the company.

"I think things around here have thrived from our close relationship and ability to anticipate each other," he adds.

"I can see that. We have a great work culture here. It was one of the things that led me to want to be a part of this company," I nod.

"Yes, and now that we have removed the cancer from around here, things will only get better," Nelson's smile grows a little more.

"Well, I hope I can fit into the subculture you two have as well," I say hopefully.

"I think you will. Detra can't fly out with us, but she has arranged to join us. I think it will be a good time for all of us to bond," he replies.

"Is there anything I should do to keep my team running here? I mean, I know the work load. I just want to make sure everything runs as usual, with all of our absence," I ask, mentally making my own checklist.

"It's December. The office will be closing in a few weeks for the holidays. Detra will meet us sometime around then. For now, everything should run smoothly. Our biggest accounts are locked in and being handled. All other bids will be taken care of in the New Year," he responds.

"Yes, so true," I nod, still tapping in a few notes on my tablet to go with the lists in my head.

"Do you mind if I remove my jacket, it's a bit warm in here?" Nelson asks, scooting forward in his seat.

My eyes take him in as he moves, his big frame taking my imagination on a trip. My eyes drop to his lap, and I damn near gasp. I lift my eyes quickly, feeling the heat in my cheeks. I'm so grateful for my darker brown skin.

"Sure, make yourself comfortable," my words come out breathily.

I pinch my eyes closed. What in the world has come over me? Okay, it's not my fault he has a print that the world can see. Damn, and what a fine print it is.

Girl, that's in a state of rest. Nelson is packing like a motherfucker. Where are my pearls?

"Would you like some water? I can have Alice bring us some," Nelson says, while I clear my lusty throat.

"No, I'm fine," I reply, but he has already sent a text.

Nelson's brows knit. "I meant to ask, would you like to do the interviews for your new assistant?"

"Oh, I had assumed Brenda would be my assistant," I respond.

Brenda was Art's secretary for as long as I've been here. I was given Art's office, so I thought I'd inherit Brenda as well. I hadn't thought very much about it to be honest.

Nelson frowns. "I'm not sure letting her stay on is such a good idea. She has a long history with Art. Lots of loyalty there," Nelson says, with a hint of anger and maybe some bitterness.

"Well, I'll use her until we find a replacement if that's okay. She knows the workload. I think she'll be fine until after the holidays. If you haven't decided to fire her yet," I say, hating the thought of anyone losing their job during the holidays.

Nelson's frown deepens. I can see him thinking over my words. He nods after a few seconds, still not seeming to like the conclusion of his thoughts. I take note of the dark shadow that crosses his face.

My interest is piqued, it's the second time I'm seeing a real hint of Nelson's temper. Something about it is kind of sexy. The broody look that dances on his face, as an internal war wages, is quite interesting.

"I guess it will be fine for now," he murmurs. "I want to start looking for her replacement as soon as we return," he says, as if giving in to some great compromise.

"Great, so let's tackle this agenda. Tell me the main focus and objects of our trip and where I can be of the most use," I say, wanting to change subjects and lighten the mood.

Alice enters the room just then with two bottled waters and two glasses. Nelson nods his thanks, but keeps his attention on me, moving right into working on the task before us.

We get so consumed in the trip and tossing around ideas, we both lose track of time. I've never been more engrossed in my job. Nelson truly is brilliant. Having someone to throw ideas back and forth with, at this level, has blown my mind.

I stretch as my back starts to stiffen. Nelson looks over his shoulder from his perch over his tablet. Again, I have to ask myself if I'm seeing things, or if that's true heat in his eyes as he gazes at me.

It's not the first time I've questioned my sanity. It seems like there has been a pull between us the entire time we've been in this office together, sitting so close to one another. I've written it off as my mind's new fascination with my boss and that monster print in his pants.

I chide my inner freak. She needs to get her shit together and mind her own business. I make a mental note to hit the spot to pick up a toy or two for the trip. This can turn into a problem over the next month or so that we're away.

Not that I would throw myself at my boss. It just wouldn't be the greatest idea to sit around in wet panties from the fantasies that have started to float in my head. It could prove to be embarrassing.

My sister Mya says Jin is a freak in the sheets. I've never dated outside my own race before. I've always been attracted to tall, dark chocolate. Every single one of my boyfriends have been over six feet and dark juicy berries. I lick my lips thinking about the berries I've had the pleasure of sucking.

Talina! You're at work, get your mind out of the gutter. You just moaned out loud.

I snap out of my dirty thoughts to see Nelson staring at me with curiosity and dare I say...desire. I want to bury my head in between the cushions of the couch. I can't believe I just zoned out like that.

"Are you hungry?" Nelson asks, in a smooth husky rasp that makes my heart skip a beat. "We've been at it for a while."

It's a simple question, but my mind goes through another series of dirty thoughts. I squeeze my thighs together. Okay, this is just nuts. I know it's been a little while, but I shouldn't be behaving like this.

I'm not exactly easy. I have only slept with boyfriends that I've been in committed relationships with. I can count them on one hand. Yet, I'm sitting here twisted up, wondering what those lips would feel like wrapped around my breast.

I clear my throat. "I think I could stand to eat something," I say softly.

"What would—" His words cutoff and he frowns down at his phone. "Shit."

"Is something wrong?" I sit up straighter when I see the tension that coils the muscles in his back.

"I don't know how this slipped my mind. I have a fundraiser tonight. My date just canceled," he purses his lips.

"Can't you take Detra?" I ask, hating the frustration that takes over his face.

"She'll already be in attendance. We're both to be auctioned off for the charity. My date was supposed to bid on me," he says, his cheeks staining with red, as he clamps his mouth shut.

I watch him closely. I see the discomfort the subject has brought on. I'm eager for more information. I have so many questions as his face goes through a range of emotions.

"Hey, I have the dress I was supposed to wear to the anniversary party. It would be a shame for it to go to waste. I'll be your date if you will have me. I can bid for you. I don't know if I can afford to outbid the other women, but I can do my best," I smile and shrug my shoulder.

The moment his eyes turn fully on me, I wish I would have kept my mouth closed. His face is shuttered, his eyes have gone hard. I don't know what I've done wrong.

~B~

Nelson

"I can bid for you. I don't know if I can afford to outbid the other women, but I can do my best."

If only she knew how much her words sting. I don't believe she'll have much competition. She wouldn't have to dig too far into her purse.

I'm a glutton for punishment. I should've waited for Detra to have free time to have this meeting. We're just short on time. We leave tomorrow evening. I've had so much on my mind, starting with my need to have Talina on this trip with me.

Spending the last few hours in this office, alone, with Talina so close, has been torture. She smells so delicious, I want to lick her to the very last drop. How does she smell like both chocolate and vanilla? More than once, I've gotten lost in fantasies of burying my face between those thick thighs.

If Talina weren't just as distracted as I've been, she would probably think me an idiot. This is a lot of change for her in a short amount of time. She must be overwhelmed. She's probably distracted with all the things she has to do before tomorrow night.

I've been trying to keep a handle on my thoughts. It's the reason for me totally forgetting to feed her. Hearing that sexy ass moan fall off her lips and seeing the distant look in her eyes reminded me we haven't eaten.

She made a similar noise when we were out eating Thai yesterday. It didn't sound as sexual, which I blame on my turn of thoughts. I've tried not to look at her like I'm ready to devour her, but I'd be lying if I said I didn't want to cup those delicious looking mounds and suck her nipples until her cum drips down those chocolate thighs.

I must be going crazy because for the last hour, I swear I can smell her arousal. I know it's all in my imagination. I want her so badly; my mind is playing tricks on me. I've been feeling this pull toward her since we sat here together.

All. In. My. Head.

"I can bid for you."

If she only knew my true reason for loathing this auction and needing a date to bid for me. Talina as my date tonight? I don't think my ego could take that.

I was so pissed off, when Detra signed me up as a bachelor to be auctioned off at the fundraiser tonight. Sometimes, I swear Detra is out to humiliate me for all the bullshit I pulled when we were teenagers.

I'd asked one of my regulars to accompany me as my date. I also gave instructions for her to drive the bid up immediately. If no one else offered a bid, I would save face. If someone did bid, but didn't offer much, I would still save face and it would all be in the name of charity.

This last minute cancellation throttles all of my plans. Now, to ask Talina to come along as my date and have to ask her to bid on me, I won't ask it. I also won't stand there and have her watch me go without a single bid.

Yes, I have money. A fortune that would drive bids alone. However, there will be eligible bachelors at the auction that have been on the covers of magazines and named in the top ten sexiest, most eligible bachelors.

I really don't know what Detra was thinking. My mother's voice has been ringing in my head since the other day when Detra dropped this bomb on me.

'Nelson, you're one ugly motherfucker. That's what I get for getting knocked up high,' my mother would hiss.

"You're one funny looking little fucker. Go get my smokes,' she'd laugh. 'Lanky ass, that nose could sniff out a secret in a vault it's so fucking big.'

'I bet the girls at school run from you. Or do they laugh in that funny looking face.' 'A face only a mother could love. Just my luck. Quit crying over that girl, she was too pretty for you anyway.' She taunted after my first girlfriend crushed my soul.

It took years for me to get over her words. To stand before a room and wait for women to bid on me. I feel sick just thinking about it. I'm going to kill Detra.

"Hola." Speaking of the devil herself, Detra floats into Talina's office, a broad smile on her lips. "Oh, God. He has that look. What kind of torture has he been putting you through?"

Talina gives a strained laugh. "He's not torturing me. I think I may have overstepped a bit," Talina replies and dips her head.

My chest squeezes. I didn't mean to make her feel as if she's the problem. Her offer just tossed me into the past. A time when I was vulnerable and so unsure of myself. My mother was a bitch. She went so far to make me feel like shit.

I rub my chest, trying to relieve some of the tightness there. I need to find the right words to turn Talina down without hurting her feelings any further. I purse my lips and pinch the bridge of my nose.

"Overstepped how?" Detra asks, gracefully flouncing in an accent chair across from us. "He can be such a bear sometimes.

I'm so sorry I can't join you in London sooner. My advice, just nod when he gets pissy. It will pass."

"You didn't overstep." I find my voice.

Detra looks between us, with wrinkled brows. "Well, what happened?"

"My date for the gala had to cancel," I huff.

"Okay, take Talina," Detra says, as if it's no big deal.

I glare at her, wanting to choke her. I narrow my eyes, when I swear I see a small smile in the corner of her lips. It's gone as she turns to Talina.

"I can have a dress sent to your place. We still have a few hours. Do you have plans tonight?" Detra persists.

"Detra," I hiss.

"I already offered. I actually have a dress, but…I'm sorry, Nelson," Talina says, before clamping her mouth shut.

"Oh, nonsense. I heard through the rumor mill that you're now single. I can add you to the roster for the auction," Detra says excited.

"No," I say with more force than I mean to.

I wince when I see Talina's head whip back. I'm only making this worse by the minute. I'm going to kill Detra.

Fuck.

Detra waves me off. "I'll have a car pick you up at seven. I'll make sure the both of you go up for auction in the first half of the night since you both have a flight to catch tomorrow," Detra insists.

"You know what, I think I'll pass. I should probably finish packing and getting ready to leave for eight weeks," Talina says quickly.

Fuck, fuck, fuck. I can see it in her eyes, I just fucked this up. I take a deep breath, knowing I'd rather be humiliated than allow Talina to think I don't want her around.

"I could truly use the date. I know it's last minute. I'll make it up to you if you would still be willing to come with me," I say, easing a smile onto my face.

Talina looks at me warily. I had planned to attend the gala, I just didn't plan to be in the auction. It is for the literacy program Talina had asked me about.

"It's for Literary Hearts, I would love for you to learn more about it," I add, trying to defuse her current caution.

"I wouldn't want you to be put out," Talina murmurs.

"I wouldn't be. I'll pick you up myself, at seven. We can ride there together," I offer. "Why let a good dress go to waste, right?"

"It's settled," Detra says, looking up from her phone. "I've already added you to the auction list."

"What?" I turn to glare at Detra.

She gives me a smug grin and a shrug. "Need to get those kids every penny we can get. Talina is gorgeous, I know she'll be able to help us meet our goal."

"I don't know about all of that," Talina gives a nervous laugh. "I'll probably bring in the lowest bid."

"I doubt that," I snort.

"Are we allowed to bid if we are in the auction?" Talina asks, I can see her eyeing me cautiously.

"Oh, but of course," Detra sings.

"Oh, that's nice," Talina replies biting her lip.

I can't help wondering what she might be thinking. I don't want her pity bids. I tighten my fists in frustration.

"This evening has just gotten so much better," Detra laugh, standing and leaving just as swiftly as she entered.

"We should call it a day. There is much to do before tonight," I say to Talina.

I won't chance a look at her. I don't know if I will even be able to after tonight. I need a drink.

CHAPTER SEVEN

Fundraiser

Talina

I'm still a bit thrown by the change in Nelson earlier. I even started to bail out of this after all. I mean, the way his demeanor changed. I still don't understand what I said or did wrong.

Maybe I insulted him with my offer to bid for him. I don't mean to imply that I was on his level or anything like that. I'm sure that my pennies won't match the bids that will come in for Nelson.

The man oozes sex. Yup, I'm blaming him for my earlier antics. My wayward thoughts and soaked panties are all his fault. Those lashes, the way his hazel eyes seem to look through you. Shit, I fan my face just thinking about it.

I know if I could, I'd break the bank for a night with him. A thought that has me once again wondering how I never noticed my boss before. It also has me thinking, why now?

"I would offer you some champagne, but I've learned my lesson," Nelson says close to my ear and my nipples tighten against the lace of my dress. "You look as nervous as I feel."

I turn my face up to get a good look at my boss. He does look nervous, which eases my nerves just a little. Questions still bounce around in my head. I asked Detra about the option to bid on others in the auction because I wanted to know if Nelson would be allowed to bid on me.

I know it's probably absolutely unethical, but a girl can dream. When the weight of the reality of the auction hit me this evening, I started to wonder who the hell would bid on me. The room is filled with mostly wealthy white men and women.

It is my biggest fear that I'll get my black ass up on that stage and no one will bid for me at all. I cringe inside, just thinking about it. My eyes land on a brother across the room.

Hope blooms until a tall blonde walks up beside him. The way she's hanging onto him, he'll be of no assistance to me this night. I'm going to kill Detra.

"I could use a Scotch right about now," I mutter.

"You have nothing to be nervous about. Look at you. I hope you don't mind me saying that you look stunning," Nelson replies.

I love this dress, it's a light shade of grey, with hues of blue, depending on how the light hits it. The lace material molds to my curves, sculpting over my breasts in a deep V. The back reflects the front with the same plunge, showing off more skin. The skirts pool at my feet in a picture of lacy elegance.

I thought it would be perfect for the anniversary party for Malcolm's parents. Sexy, but elegant. Something to show off what my man could be proud to say was his.

Now, standing in this room, with tons of wealthy women that brought their A game, I feel empowered in the graceful drape of the dress. I work hard for this body, it's not surgeon manufactured. Something I think I would have a hard time saying about ninety percent of the guests here.

"Thank you, Nelson," I say, feeling my cheeks burn and lowering my lashes. "I don't mind at all. You look very handsome yourself."

"This will be good practice for London. We'll have plenty of elbow rubbing to do there. I'll need you to join me for a few dinners and balls such as this," he replies, with disdain written on his face as he looks around.

"Not your scene?" I chuckle. I also note he glossed over my compliment. Again, I think I overstepped.

"I'm a dirty white boy from Jersey. I never in my life thought I'd be here. This is all Detra. She made connections that opened doors." Nelson shrugs.

My antennas go up. I'm sensing more to that story. To my disappointment, Nelson switches gears again.

"Are you sure you're up for the auction? Your break up is still fresh. I can have you removed," Nelson offers, his hazel eyes, soft, but sharp, as he looks into mine.

"It's for a good cause. Besides, it was time for Malcolm and I to move on," I lift a shoulder.

"Nelson," a voice booms to my left.

I turn to see a very handsome gentleman stopping to join our little party. He's the epitome of movie star gorgeous, green eyes, dark hair, a square jaw, high cheekbones. He has those sexy bedroom eyes. He's definitely a ten.

"Jack, how are you?" Nelson says, placing a possessive hand on the small of my back.

I promise you, my thong is liquefied with the simple touch. My brows draw in, never in my life, and I mean never, has this happened to me. I look up at Nelson, but if he's aware of the fact that he has me wetter than a slip and slide, he shows no signs of it.

I do my damnedest not to melt into his touch. Instead, I force my gaze back to Jack and his handsome looks. I look at the man, waiting to see if his presence will send my mind on a dirty journey, as Nelson has done all day.

Nothing.

"Now, who do we have here?" Jack says, beaming down at me.

Nope, not a thing, and his voice happens to be very pleasant. As handsome as he is, and as smooth as that voice is, I feel nothing. It's Nelson's rumbling rasp that has my nipples straining.

"This is Talina. My date," Nelson replies. I blink, as I think I detect a hint of warning in Nelson's tone.

"Ah, I believe I saw your name on the auction board. Talina Valentine. I thought it lovely and unusual," Jack smiles. "Now that I've put a face to the name, I'm all the more intrigued."

"Too bad you're in the auction. You won't have time to bid," Nelson says tightly.

"Oh, I plan to find time. It's for charity after all, isn't it?" Jack smiles.

"Yes, that it is," I nod and give a small smile.

Jack seems to be nice enough. Although, he's not very covert about his gaze lingering on my breasts. His eyes move back up to mine, causing me to lift a brow at him. The corners of his lips turn up into a dangerous smile.

I bet that look gets him plenty. I'm just not trying to be next. Something tells me Jack isn't one to stick around after.

Jack takes my hand and lifts it to his lips. "To an evening that has just gotten better," he breathes against my skin.

"It's time for an auction," Detra says, as she floats over, breaking up a moment that has just started to feel a little too tense.

I can feel the rigid stance of Nelson beside me. When I look up into his face, he's watching me closely. His eyes are hard, just like earlier. Again, I feel like I did something wrong.

"Let's go, you two. You can win each other and put out that fire later," Detra mutters.

"What?" I turn to her, puzzled.

"I said, let's go get those kids some money." Detra smiles.

~B~

Nelson

That dress is going to drive me insane. Every man here has been murmuring about the chocolate goddess on my arm tonight. I truly don't believe Talina knows how beautiful she is.

I seriously am going to kill Detra. I want to sweep Talina into my arms and run off with her. The hungry look that Jack gave her made me want to tear his head off.

Now, I stand here watching a room full of men, giving Talina the same hungry look as she walks out onto the stage in that fucking dress. She looks like a dream as she walks out with her head held high.

It's at this moment that it all clicks. Talina is the woman of my dreams. It's the reason I can't seem to stop obsessing over her. It's why I become unglued when it comes to her. I haven't dared to dream about anyone since having my heart shattered so many years ago.

Wanting someone like Talina places me in a vulnerable place that I hate. Memories I won't allow to surface claw at the door of my mind. The door I slammed shut and won't allow to open ever again.

"We will start the bidding with five hundred dollars," the MC announces.

I clinch my jaw. I should leave, I don't think I can sit here and watch this, but I'm riveted to the front of the stage, where Talina is standing. She looks nervous, but a smile is plastered on her glossed lips.

"Five thousand," is called from the center of the room.

I ball my fist in the tablecloth, my jaw clenching. Talina's mouth falls open. She actually looks surprised. I'm astonished that she had any doubts.

"Ten thousand," a deeper voice calls.

My entire being stiffens. I can feel the sweat on my brow. She's my employee. I just gave her a promotion. I shouldn't bid.

"You know you can bid on her," Detra whispers in my ear. "It's for charity. I know you don't want anyone else to win a private date with her."

"I'm going to ring your neck," I hiss.

"Fifteen thousand," a third bidder calls.

"Nelson, stop being a pussy. Bid," Detra hisses back.

"Twenty-Five," another bidder throws in his hat.

"One hundred thousand," I stand and call out.

Talina's head snaps in my direction. Her cheeks look flushed, her chest begins to heave. I swallow hard. Have I just made a mistake?

"Five hundred thousand," a voice, I know too well, calls.

I turn to glare at Jack. His eyes are locked on Talina. I want to punch him in the throat. "One million," I say through my teeth.

A gasp from the stage catches my attention. I turn to see Talina staring back at me. Her brows are knitted tightly and her chest is now heaving so hard it looks like it's going to burst from her gown.

Fuck, does she want Jack to outbid me? Is she about to panic because I'm bidding for her? I look down at the tablecloth and begin to lower back into my seat.

"Don't you fucking dare," Detra says, like a little devil on my shoulder.

"One point five," Jack says smugly.

"Leave it alone," I say and close my eyes.

~B~
Talina

I don't know what the hell just happened. I didn't think anyone would bid on me. One point five million dollars? A million and a half dollars for a date with *me*?

I can't even wrap my head around that. Yet, that's not the thought that's screaming at the forefront of my mind. *Why the hell isn't Nelson still bidding? Is the price too steep?*

"One point five million, going once," the MC announces.

I ball my fists into gown, willing Nelson to look up at me. I didn't think he would bid at all, but now that he has. I want that date. I want him to win.

"Going twice," The MC continues the countdown.

To my own surprise. I close my eyes and say a prayer. He can't stop bidding now. Not yet.

Please, Nelson, don't give up on me.

~B~
Nelson

"Since when are you a quitter? What you want is right within your grasp. You give up now then they win, everything they did…they succeeded in breaking you," Detra says in a haunted tone.

"Leave it," I growl in response.

"Damn it, Nelson. If you don't bid I will," Detra snaps. "I'll take your girl and turn her ass out. You know I will. I haven't had a threesome in a while."

"Going twice," The MC calls.

Detra's earlier words have already rattled my cage. I'm not worried about her threat, but the thought of someone else out bidding me for what's mine. I won't have it.

I lift my head and stand to my feet once again, straightening to my full height. I've conquered obstacle after obstacle in my life. Detra's right, I can't let them win.

I lock my eyes on the woman I want. Her head is down, I would swear she's praying. It's enough that I almost take a pause, but I don't. Not tonight, not this time.

"Three million dollars," I boom through the room, stopping the entire auction on its head.

~B~

Talina

I lift my head to collective gasps, as the words, *Three million dollars,* rock me to my core. My eyes lock with Nelson's instantly. I can't close my mouth.

The fire in Nelson's eyes reveals something new. He seems to be standing taller, his shoulders straighter. The determination rolling off of him seems to have a weight of its own.

"Wow, folks, do we have another bid. Three million and one perhaps?" the MC says, sounding as stunned as I am.

Nelson keeps his gaze locked on me, seeming to be watching for my reaction. I haven't been able to move a muscle. I'm frozen in shock.

"Well, then, three million going once, going twice, gone. Young lady, that dress has brought in a lot of money for these wonderful kids," the MC teases, while coming to my side.

I remember to breathe, letting it swoosh past my lips. It hits me that Nelson just bid three million dollars on me.

Holy shit!

I let a smile stretch across my face, as I look up through my lashes at Nelson. I watch as a cocky smile starts slow on his lips. It's sexy as fuck.

Well, damn.

CHAPTER EIGHT

Bubbling

Talina

I walk off the stage in a daze. The backstage coordinator is talking to me, but I don't hear a word. I'm still in shock. I feel like I'm floating in a dream.

A bidding war, for *me*? I can't believe any of it. Three million dollars. I'm not even sure how to take what just happened. I mean, what does it mean?

"Here, take this, honey. You look a little pale," the coordinator says, handing me a glass of Champagne.

I take the Champagne and down it without thinking. I place the glass on a nearby table and rub my temples. A tray passes with Hors d'oeuvres and I reach for a few. I know I should have asked what the little bites are that I'm shoveling into my mouth, but my brain is just not firing the way it should be.

"Hope I can come close to your numbers," A handsome blonde says, with a wink, as he passes me by for the stage.

"Three million dollars," I whisper like a nitwit.

"Yes, honey. You pulled in three million. Jack Knight didn't look none too pleased either, I thought he was going to counter," the coordinator says.

Her red glasses perch low on her nose, as she looks me over. She's looking at me as if she's trying to find out what's so special about me, how I warranted such a high bid. She doesn't know that I'm trying to figure the same thing out.

I snag two more Hors d'oeuvres as the tray passes again. I eat when I'm stressed. As much as I wanted Nelson to win, I now have so many questions and thoughts running through my head.

Why in the world did Nelson bid so much money for me? This is his charity. Maybe he won't have to cough up the cash. Will he seriously take me on a date? Why was he so pissy about me being his date earlier, if he was going to turn around and bid three million dollars for me?

"There you are," Detra says, as she appears. "Nelson was concerned about you. Everything alright?"

"Yes," I press out. "I think I'm just in shock."

Detra pulls a face looking at me like I'm crazy. "Did you or did you not look in the mirror before you left the house?" Detra frowns at me. "I swear you two make no sense."

"Huh?" I wrinkle my brows.

"Nothing, come on. He will shut this thing down if we don't turn up soon," Detra sighs.

"I haven't completed getting all of Ms. Valentine's information for the date," the coordinator pouts.

"I got it, Andrea. Give it a rest," Detra tosses over her shoulder.

Detra pulls me closer and leans into my ear. "That chick is weirder than glowing cat shit," she whispers.

I cover my mouth, as a laugh bubbles up. I nudge Detra for making me laugh so suddenly. She just gives me a look and shrugs.

It hits me that I can get some answers from her. I stop, placing a hand on Detra's arm. She pauses and gives me a quizzical look.

"Can I ask you something?" I whisper, looking around at all the other people moving about.

"Of course. Is everything okay?" She replies with concern in her eyes.

I wring my hands before me. "Does Nelson usually place a bid so high?" I chew on my lip, after asking the question.

Detra gives me a mischievous smile. "He never bids. He writes a check at the end of the night," she answers. "Although, those checks are never as high."

"Sh...should, I bid for him. I know I won't be able to outbid the others, but should I at least try? Do you think it would look bad, him being my boss and all?" I stammer.

Detra sighs. "He won't be up for auction. Fucker had me pull him at the last damn minute," Detra twists her lips.

I wrinkle my brows. "But he would have brought in so much money," I say in confusion.

"You and I know that," Detra shakes her head. "Listen, we better get back. We'll get into the mind of Nelson some other time. I'm sure you will have loads of questions after London and *your date.*"

Her last words are said with a saucy hint to them and a smile that takes over her face. While amusing, I also feel like Detra isn't saying something. I let that thought go, as out of nowhere my stomach begins to cramp a little.

I let Detra take a few steps in front of me before looking around to make sure the coast is clear. Seeing no one in the corridor, I squeeze out a little wind, praying it will remain a silent one.

Crap, what the hell did I eat. I place a finger under my nose and run from my own smell. *Please don't let that have been shrimp or any type of seafood,* I pray in my head. My stomach has no tolerance for the stuff. Seafood runs right through me.

I wish I would've asked what those appetizers where. Oh, God, did I drink Champagne too? Note to self, get some water in your system.

~B~

Nelson

I wasn't completely sure I made the right decision, not until the look Talina gave me when the bid was final. The way she looked at me through her lashes, made me reassess everything. I know that look.

It's the look I get after fucking the shit out of one of my dates. It's the look I get when the shock wears off and they want more. The moment they realize good looks doesn't equate great sex.

The moment they begin to desire me as a man, not a potential shopping spree or payday. Only Talina has never had me between her legs to eat her soul out through her pussy. She has yet to learn that I'll dick her down until she can't breathe, but still can't stop begging for more.

She knows none of that, but that look in her eyes read desire, a desire for me. I want to see her up close. I want to see that look in her eyes, when I'm looking down at her.

It's why I sent Detra looking for Talina. I didn't expect her to take so long coming from back stage. The nagging voices in the back of my head try to tell me Talina is second-guessing what just happened.

I shut those voices down, just like I had to do to climb my way out of the pit of a life I had as a kid. So much has changed. I can't subscribe to the bullshit that used to be my past. I refuse to, which means from here moving forward I'll be as aggressive about pursuing Talina as I've been about everything else in my life.

"I found her," Detra announces, as she and Talina return to the table.

I take notice that Talina lags behind a little. My chest begins to pound. There's a little frown on her face, her hands are clenching her stomach.

"Are you okay?" I lean to whisper in her ear, as I pull out her chair.

"Um, yes," she replies, but her face says otherwise.

I reclaim my seat, after Talina takes hers. I try not to stare as I see the discomfort on her face. Could I really have imagined it all?

I must have because she won't even look at me now. I watch as sweat begins to dew on her forehead. Her hand goes up to cover her face, while she looks down into her lap.

The auction is still going on in the background, but I can't pull my eyes from Talina. I should've kept my mouth shut. My mother was right. I will always be the fool for a pretty face.

"Is everything okay?" Detra leans over me to ask Talina.

"Yes, yes, I...I just. I'm not feeling too well," Talina says, making a face.

"Would you like to go home? I can call the car around," I offer.

"I don't want to ruin the evening," she says softly.

"If you are unwell, we can call it a night," I say tightly.

I'm trying to hide my frustration and failing terribly. I clench and unclench my fists under the table. I can command a boardroom, know the exact moment I'm going to close a deal, but I can't read the one woman that matters most to me.

I should have never bid for Talina. I've just created an awkward situation for everyone. Look at her, she won't even look at me.

"Oh, excuse me," Talina says, standing quickly.

"Fuck," I hiss under my breath, when she's gone.

"Stop over thinking things," Detra says next to me.

"She can't stand to sit next to me. I shouldn't have bid for her," I mutter.

"Nelson, you have got to stop waiting for the other shoe to drop. You've learned over the years, nothing is as we perceive it to be. Just relax," Detra huffs.

"Um," I respond.

We sit through three more volunteers being auctioned off, and still there's no sign of Talina. My stomach knots with each passing minute. I've berated myself a hundred times in the last fifteen minutes.

"That's it, I'm going to find her," I lean in to murmur into Detra's ear.

"Nelson," she calls my name, as I get up and move from the table.

I have no idea what I plan to say to Talina once I find her. I just know I'm not going to sit and let this continue. If she wants the date with Jack Knight, I'll set them up.

~*B*~

Talina

This is so embarrassing. This has to be the worst night of my life. That had to be some type of seafood. I gobbled them down so fast, I don't even remember what they taste like.

I wince as I cut wind and release another wave of shit. It hasn't let up. Sweats pouring from my face, I have my dress balled up in my hands, and I'm sitting on a public toilet covered in doubled sheets of toilet paper.

I almost didn't get the toilet covered in time. I'm just happy I made it into the bathroom in the first place. If I would have sat at that table a moment longer.

I groan, my stomach cramps and my butt seems to answer my groan. I call on all sorts of baby Jesus and angels to make this stop, but it doesn't. I don't know if it ever will.

"Ma'am are you okay in there," I hear through the stall door.

Just my luck. There would be a bathroom attendant at an event like this. I can't even shit in peace.

How did I go from feeling like a beautiful princess at the ball, to this? Oh, God, I'm on a date. Not officially, but I'm sure after this, Nelson won't want that three-million-dollar date.

"I'm fine," I moan.

"Okay, Miss," I hear the attendant reply.

On second thought, I may need a little favor. My shoulders sag, as I think of what I'm about to do. My stomach seems like it's going to finally allow me to move from this seat.

"Excuse me," I call out softly.

"Yes, ma'am."

"I'm going to ask you a favor. I will pay you five hundred dollars after," I say and hold my breath for an answer.

"Okay, what can I do?" I hear, after a brief pause.

"I need you to make sure no one else comes into this bathroom. I need you to step outside the door and tell them it's out of order," I say, my brows raised in hopes she will agree.

"Um, okay," she says, after a longer pause this time.

I close my eyes in relief. This is so fucking embarrassing, but there's no way I'm leaving this bathroom without washing my ass. No way in hell.

I roll toilet paper around my hand and clean myself up as best I can. Reaching down, I pull my thong from around my ankles, balling it into my free hand. I stand and the toilet automatically flushes. Lifting my foot, I kick the toilet paper covering inside. I still have my gown bunched up around my waist. With my dress still in my grasp, I open the stall door and peek out.

I sigh when I don't see anyone inside the bathroom. I rush to the sink, where I noticed the attendant's basket of fresh hand towels. I snatch one and do my best to juggle my dress and thong in one hand, and the towel in the other.

I hold the towel under the faucet, since it's one of the hands free ones. However, nothing comes out. I huff and start to wave my hand under the sink. Panic fills me as the water still doesn't run.

I lift the back of my hand to my forehead and inhale. Wrong move. I've lit this place up. Frustrated, I try to hold the towel under the water again. Finally, the water starts to run.

Once the towel is wet, I reach over to allow the soap to run onto the fabric. I go to town cleaning my behind. This soap is probably going to chafe my ass, but at this point it's better than nothing.

Someday, I will look back on this mess and laugh at myself. Tonight, I just want to go home and cry. Once I'm clean enough for me and my mother's standards, I slip on my thong and smooth out my dress as best I can.

I need to phone a friend. I would love to be beamed right out of this bathroom into my own home. I shake my head at that thought. I still need to get to my purse to pay the attendant that five hundred.

I toss the towel in the trash and wash my hands for good measure. I dab at my face with a fresh towel and discard it in the proper soiled linens basket. Looking in the mirror, I know this is as good as it's going to get.

With my stomach still bubbling, I know I need to get out of here. I rush out of the door to find the attendant looking a bit frazzled. My cheeks heat with embarrassment.

"Thank you so much," I say. "I need to go get my purse. I promise I'll be right back."

"What do you need your purse for?" I hear rumbled behind me. I close my eyes and want to crawl into myself.

What did I do to deserve this?

~B~

Nelson

At this point, I figured Talina was trying to cut out on me. Memories try to break through my barrier, but I won't let them. I will not stoop to feeling like that kid so many years ago.

"Here's your purse," Detra says from behind me.

"Oh, thank you," Talina responds.

She looks nervous and as she should be, embarrassed. She was the one that offered to accompany me tonight. I can't believe this is how the night has turned out. I had been optimistic when I first saw her step out of her building in her gown. So much for that.

"I'm sorry, I'm having a bit of a feminine issue. I'm going to have to call it a night," Talina says, clutching her purse to her chest.

"Detra will see you home," I snap and spin on my heels.

I was wrong, she's just like all the rest. It's better I know it now. I'll never repeat the past.

CHAPTER NINE

You Called

Talina

This first two weeks here in London have been interesting to say the least. Nelson hasn't brought up the auction once. Not that he talks to me much outside of details for work. It's been this way since we boarded the plane to come here.

Nelson has been distant. He speaks mostly when he has something to say about the work we're doing here in London. Which, by the way, is so much more than I was prepared for. Nelson is pure genius.

Our company deals mostly with marketing, but this expansion will turn Fisher, Inc. into a marketing, branding, and product development giant. We'll be able to tell our clients what they need, instead of them bringing what they think they need to us.

Nelson has already taken two British companies and revamped their business models to freshen up their companies. It's not always about the big idea, but how to make the core of the idea work.

Nelson has taken companies that have lost their focus and shown them what their consumers truly want. It's amazing. We have such great expectations for the first quarter of the year.

I wish I could say my expectations were as high for my relationship with Nelson. I miss the easy-going boss I got to connect with back in New York. Things have been very different over the last two weeks.

I wouldn't mind so much if I weren't with him for what seems to be twenty-four-seven. I'd thought we were going to be staying in a hotel for the eight weeks we'll be here in London. However, to my surprise, the first night we arrived at a private home, owned by Nelson.

The elegant brownstone is stunning, but the close quarters feel awkward. I feel like there are so many unanswered questions between us. I still haven't a clue why he would bid so much money for me. Especially now, as he freezes me out.

I expected to spend this trip away from my family for the holiday, just not under this tension. I know it's just Mya now. Well, Mya and Jin, but spending this time with them would've been better than walking on eggshells here.

I thought this trip would be exciting and fun. I know it's a work situation, but I didn't expect it to become depressing. Nelson has been treating me more and more like I'm the one responsible for kicking his puppy.

He is never rude. Well, I'll take that back. When we are here in the brownstone, alone, Nelson can be quite dismissive. He won't stay in a room alone with me for more than five seconds. He's become brooding and snippy.

Yet, I can't for the life of me stop having these fantasies and daydreams about him. At this point, his presence is just getting on my damn nerves. I don't know if I want to ask him what his damn problem is, or throw him against the nearest wall, jump on his waist, and hump his brains out.

Nelson just looks strong enough to hold all this up and still keep pounding. Ugh, my brain has been wondering over thoughts like that since I woke up this morning. It's Christmas Eve, so there's no work today.

An idle mind is a dangerous thing. Being busy with work has kept me from circling my thoughts of Nelson. However, this morning, as my ears are greeted with the harshness of my own breathing and the ramblings of my own mind, I can't stop thinking of what that print I've noticed repeatedly would feel like.

"Ugh," I growl and punch the bed beneath me.

I roll onto my stomach and bury my face into the pillow. Squeezing my thighs together, I try not to think of Nelson yesterday morning after his run. His hair damp, his torso sweaty and shirtless, those grey sweatpants, and the determination that oozed from him.

I wish I knew what he was so determined about. The focused look in his eyes more than piqued my interest. I guess it's a good thing he has a live-in housekeeper here. Ms. Cork saved me from jumping Nelson right where he stood and embarrassing myself. Living here with Nelson, I've never been concerned for my own safety, it's his safety that I question.

"What's wrong with you?" I huff into my pillow. "Shit, I need to take the edge off."

I'm talking to my horny self. I need help. I'll be glad when Detra arrives. She should be here after Christmas. She informed me she would be spending the holidays with her family.

"Just a few more days," I murmur to myself.

Yet, even her presence isn't going to do anything for my needs. *Has it been that long?* I truly think it has.

I give in. Like a thief in the night, I sit up and creep over to the closet. I retrieve my suitcase for the few items I didn't unpack.

I bite my lip, as I look at my options. At this point, I'm not in the mood to drag this out. I make a quick decision, moving the suitcase back to the closet.

My We-Vibe will get me there nice and quick. My mind turns back to a sweat soaked Nelson. His muscled back and the fluid movement of that tall body of his.

I wiggle free of my panties, switch on my vibrator, and get to work. A long sigh spills from my lips. I picture those hazel eyes and long lashes staring back at me. I can feel those full lips wrapped around my nipple, sweat dripping from his nose onto my skin.

I buck off the bed, crying out. I completely lose myself in my own pleasure. I reach to cup my breast, as I feel my peak rushing further.

"Fuck, yes," I whimper. My orgasm hits so hard, I start to call his name, while I drown in mindless bliss.

Suddenly, my perfect release is interrupted by a knock on the door. I nearly jump out of my skin. My heart pounds in my chest. My mind clears enough to register that I may have been a little louder than I meant to be.

"Shit," I whisper, my face turning hot with embarrassment. "Just a second," I call out.

I drop the vibrator and jump off the bed. My eyes dart around the room. I spot my robe, rushing to put it on. I groan when I go to tie it shut, but the tie is missing.

Another knock sounds on the door, and I stomp my foot in frustration. Tugging the robe closed, I wrap my arms around my waist. I cross the room and crack the door open.

My eyes meet with a white t-shirt covered chest, not the kind blue eyes I was hoping for. Ms. Cork is a tiny thing, a little shorter than me. I was praying it would be her on the other side of the door.

My eyes slowly lift to the hazel eyes staring back down at me. I watch as his nostrils flare, and his eyes darken. Yet, Nelson's face gives nothing else away. I switch my prayer to hoping I wasn't as loud as I think I was.

I want to slap my forehead. I have no idea what I was thinking. Why on earth had I been calling this man's name?

I shift at the thick awkward silence between us, as he continues to stare in my eyes. The movement seems to catch his attention. His eyes drag down to my breasts like a hot caress. My nipples pebble against the silk of my robe.

I swallow hard trying to find words, but I have none. I tighten my fingers in the silky fabric, feeling as if I'm completely naked. I would swear his gaze could see right through the thin material.

When his words fill the air, I feel them in my core. Never in my life have the simplest of words made me so wet and filled with need. My entire being stands to attention.

~B~

Nelson

I'm uncomfortable in my own space. I hate this tension between us. I've kept my distance from Talina. I still don't believe her words from the night of the fundraiser. She lied and I know she did. I haven't been able to move past that.

Detra tried her best to tell me there was more going on with Talina. I'm just not willing to throw myself under that bus. I'm better off walking away. Just as I should be doing right now.

Walking away from those big, brown doe eyes. I'd come to her door to knock and see if she wanted to have breakfast with me. I know I've been freezing her out. I figured I'd try to be more pleasant with it being Christmas Eve.

What I wasn't expecting was the sounds coming from inside her room. The sexy erotic sounds that have me swollen inside my jeans. Then, I heard her calling my name.

Fuck, I sure as hell wasn't expecting her to open the door in nothing but a robe. I can smell her. I lick my lips with the thought, as I stare at her pebbled nipples.

"You called?" I say, watching her swallow hard, as her chest heaves.

My eyes lift back to hers. They're wide with what seems to be surprise or shock. Her pupils are completely blown. It's that desire I was sure I saw on her face that night I bid for her. The moment I'd been confident that she wanted me, as much as I want her.

But what happened once she got off the stage? What changed? Something had changed and it wasn't a fucking feminine issue.

"I...I, um, I was talking on the phone," she says breathlessly.

I purse my lips and grit my teeth. She's lying to me again. I'll tolerate a lot, but I will not tolerate being lied to.

I step into her space, bumping the door open a little further with my shoulder. I dip my head so we're eye to eye. Talina's hand reaches out, resting on my chest. It's not a restraining motion. It seems to be more of a gesture to help her stay up right.

"We're going to stop with the lies, Talina. I don't like being lied to," I say tightly.

Her brows draw in. "I don't lie to you. When have I lied to you?"

"Other than a moment ago. You lied to me at the gala," I reply.

Her eyes search mine, then a look of realization and embarrassment enters her eyes. I'm thrown when she places her forehead on my chest. I feel her body shake, and at first, I think I've made her cry.

My arms go around her on instinct, but that's when I hear her laughter. I reach to pinch her chin between my fingers and lift her face to my view. Tears are spilling down her cheeks, but there's mirth in her eyes.

"Please tell me that's not the reason you've been so cold to me," she laughs.

"I don't find it funny. I have a serious problem with being lied to," I say more roughly than I mean to.

She barks out more laughter. I hate the way my chest squeezes at the sound. Her face glows with the laughter that's now shaking her soft body against mine.

"Oh, God, Nelson. You have no idea how terrible that night was for me," I stiffen at her words. "I had a reaction to something I ate. Detra confirmed that the appetizers were indeed seafood."

The blood drains from my face. "You're allergic to seafood," I breathe out. Talina throws her head back with more laughter. I watch her, as my mind travels back to that night to confirm her words. "Wait, how do you know that?" She tilts her head at me.

"I offered you some of my curry shrimp. You told me you couldn't stomach seafood. You react to it as if you have food poisoning," I remember the conversation aloud.

"I was embarrassed. I just wanted to go home," she says sheepishly.

I nod, now understanding that night a little better. I stare into her eyes thinking. So much wasted time over a misunderstanding.

It isn't until Talina releases a soft moan, that I realize that I've allowed my hands to roam down to her plump ass. Her breasts press into my chest, and I harden even more against her belly.

Her arms are now wrapped around my waist. I flex my fingers, drawing her into my body. Her eyes tell me of her desire for me.

"Nelson, can I ask you something?" she says softly.

"Yes," I rumble.

"Why did you bid three million dollars for me?"

"Because I want you for myself. I wasn't going to allow anyone to bid for what's mine," I answer without thinking.

Talina licks her lips and nods her head. "Interesting," she replies, as her arms reach up to wrap around my neck. Her fingers go into my hair, tugging me down towards her.

My heart starts to pound in my chest. My eyes zone in on her full lips as they come closer and closer. I feel the heat that rushes my body the moment her pillow soft lips press to mine.

Something in me snaps. I lift my hands to cup her face and hold her to me as I devour her face. I kiss her deeply, surveying her mouth for every detail and surface. She tastes of mint and chocolate.

The chocolates I had Ms. Cork place in her room. It's a rich and decadent flavor. I groan as her scent fills my head, a combination of her essence and something citrusy. I move my hands back to her ass, lifting her onto my waist.

Her legs lock around me like she'd been waiting to do so for a lifetime. Clinging tightly to me, I can feel the heat from her core scorching my abs.

I move into the bedroom swiftly, not wanting my staff to see us in the hallway. I use my bare foot to close the door behind us. We don't break the kiss, as I make my way to the bed.

I place Talina on the bed, moving over her. I press into her lightly, letting her feel me. When I finally break the kiss, I lift to look down at her.

My hands move to part the fabric of her silk robe, I reach to run the backs of my fingers against her breast. Her skin feels just as soft as the robe. I watch her flesh goose bump beneath my touch.

"So fucking gorgeous," I murmur. "I've dreamt of a million ways to fuck you. I want to hear my name come from your lips again, but this time I want to be the direct reason for your pleasure."

"Nelson, please," she whimpers, when I pinch her nipple.

"I like begging, baby," I respond.

"Please," she breathes.

"Good girl," I purr and dip my head.

Her sweetness bursts on my tongue, as I suck her tight bud into my mouth. I knead the mound that I'm worshiping with my lips, dragging a divine sound from hers.

"Nelson," she gasps. It's music to my ears. If I'm dreaming I don't ever want to wake.

~B~

Talina

Can you have a heart attack by orgasm? I swear, it feels like he is going to suck my heart from my chest through my breast. I know I'm soaking the front of his jeans as I rock my hips against him.

I'm so wet. I need more, but I'm afraid to ask him to change routes. I don't want to lose this feeling. I'm so close, my head is buzzing on overload. His strong hand grasps my waist, pinning me to the bed.

It's just the right amount of pressure, not too rough, but not gentle at all. Nelson's touch is possessive, as if meant to demonstrate his intention to own this body. Oh, and damn, is he owning my body with only a simple touch and his mouth.

I see stars as he presses his hips into me a little harder, and sucks just a bit stronger. I throw my head back, buck into him, and cry out. I'm keening so loudly I barely hear the sound of my phone ringing on the nightstand.

I ignore it, while I bask in the feel of Nelson's hands on my body. He drags his lips to my other breast and begins the same assault all over again. I'm all for it. In fact, he could start it a little lower, or skip that all together and get naked.

Unfortunately, my bliss is broken when my phone rings again. My head clears a bit, as my sister comes to mind. It's around three in the morning back home.

I groan, pushing up on my elbows. "Wait, that could be my sister," I breath out.

Nelson groans, placing his head against the center of my chest. I reach over for my phone. Panic fills my chest when I see it is indeed my sister calling. I pick up quickly.

"Mya, is everything okay?" I rush out.

"Oh, my God, Oh, my God, oh, my God," Mya rushes into the phone.

"Mya, what is it? What's wrong?" I call back.

"It's three in the freaking morning. How was I supposed to know he was bringing his family back to the house?" Mya moans into the phone.

"Mya, what's going on?"

"I'll never be able to look them in the face ever again. Jin said they were going to a hotel. I…I…shit, Talina. What am I going to do?" My sister panics.

"First, you need to calm down. Then, I need you to tell me what the heck is going on," I say firmly.

"Jin's parents missed their original flight. He went to pick them up after they caught a red eye. They were supposed to be staying at a hotel. I had planned all of this before they missed the flight. I didn't know," Mya nearly sobs.

"Didn't know what? Planned what?" I say, getting frustrated with my sister.

"I didn't know they would be coming here. I thought Jin was just going to drop them at the hotel and come back home," Mya explains, as if I'm dense.

"Okay, well, what the hell happened that has you freaking out?" I snap at her.

"I had planned to give Jin his Christmas present when he returned," she whimpers.

"O…kay, still lost here," I sigh.

"I was his Christmas present. I dressed in a pair of red heels, a red thong, and wrapped my damn boobs in a red ribbon. Our house is on gated private property.

"I thought I'd meet him in the driveway when he pulled up. He was supposed to be the only freaking one in the car," Mya whines.

"No, Mya…wait, it has to be brick ass there, you went out in the cold like that?" I bite back a laugh.

"I didn't expect to be out there long and my man was going to warm me up. Oh, God, Talina. That's not even the worst part," Mya whines.

"I couldn't see everyone in the car because of the headlights. When Jin turned them off, I freaked the fuck out. I turned and hauled ass for the house, only to find out I locked my dumbass out of the house.

"There I was, ass out, with my boyfriend's Asian family piled in the car. His mother, father, grandmother, and little brother. Oh, my God, Talina," Mya cries out.

Sorry, not sorry. I burst into laughter and fall back on the bed. At this point, I'd forgotten all about Nelson, who rolled onto his back beside me.

I peek over at him and he's watching me closely. I roll my lips in and try to stop laughing. Tears slide from my eyes. If you think crazy shit happens to me, my sister has cornered the market on this stuff.

"Mya, honey, you can't stay locked in the bathroom forever," I hear Jin's voice say gently, through the phone.

"Mya, you're locked in the bathroom?" I snort.

"You suck," Mya hisses into the phone. "What am I going to do?"

"Girl, they know your ass is crazy. They also know you're crazy about that man. Suck it up and get your ass out there.

"Make your guests feel at home and then put it on your man like you planned to," I chuckle. "It will all blow over in the morning," I shrug, as if she can see me.

"That's easy for you to say. Your boyfriend's mother doesn't look at you like the world's biggest thief," Mya grumbles.

"You did steal that woman's son," I giggle.

"Why did I call you?" Mya sighs.

"Because I'm the best little sister in the world," I chirp.

"Um, whatever, hey, maybe you should call Malcolm. He called me the other day. He didn't sound right," Mya changes the subject.

I can still hear Jin trying to coax her out of the bathroom. I press a hand to my forehead. I don't for the life of me understand why Malcolm would be calling my sister. I also don't know why she's advocating for him. The two have always disliked each other.

I turn to look at Nelson, as the temperature in the room seems to drop. He shifts his body to the edge of the bed and stands. I want to tell him to wait, but I don't want my sister in my business.

I cover the phone. "Nelson," I whisper, but he doesn't respond.

"Mya, I'll call you later," I say to my sister.

"Ta, I don't like you two as a couple, but I just think you should call him. He's always been your friend. Call him as a friend," Mya says softly.

"Yeah, I got it," I sigh, watching Nelson's back, as he leaves my room.

Back to square one.

CHAPTER TEN

Need to Know

Talina

It's been a long day. I haven't seen Nelson since this morning. I know he heard me when I called his name. If he heard my sister mention Malcolm, he heard me whisper his name.

I want to know what he's thinking. While I want to finish what we started, I want to get to know Nelson as well. I can't ignore what I've been feeling around him. From his words and actions earlier, he must feel something for me as well.

"Nelson," I call softly, causing him to lift his head to lock eyes with me. "I waited for you in the dining room."

"I had some things I wanted to look over," he points down at the papers before him on the large oak desk.

His home office is something right out of a movie. The large desk, the bookshelves and expensive paintings on the walls. It screams Detra's finesse. I get that about them. Detra places a finesse on all things Nelson.

I don't understand it, but I see it. From what I know they come from the same past, but they've both changed their lives for the better. I admire that.

"It's Christmas Eve," I say.

Nelson's eyes regard me closely. I watch as his thoughts flash across his face. He stands, moves around the desk, and leans his butt against the front.

I move closer, stopping right before him. I reach to caress his jaw. His eyes close, his large hand coming up to cover mine.

"Talk to me, Nelson," I plea. "I thought I felt a connection earlier. Am I wrong?"

His eyes open and lock with mine. "Are you over your relationship with your ex?" He asks bluntly.

I wrinkle my brows, weighing his words for myself. "Malcolm? He'll always be a friend. I spent five years of my life with him, but that chapter of my life is over. I guess you can say I'm over it." I shrug.

"No, Talina, I don't want you to guess." Nelson shakes his head. "I need you to know. I'm not looking to just sleep with you. I want you. I never thought you would be available for me to have. I need to know if you're available."

"I know I'm over him," I reply, moving in closer. "I'm available, Nelson. Maybe…maybe, we should slow things down. Get to know each other. That way you'll be more comfortable when you see I've moved on."

Nelson licks his lips and nods curtly. "Slow, that sounds good," he says through a tight jaw.

I grin up at him. "Are you sure?"

"Yes," he sighs, dipping his head to place his forehead to mine. "Did you eat without me?"

"No. Besides, don't I owe you a three-million-dollar date," I laugh.

Nelson seems to relax when I wrap my arms around him. "Yes, you do. Do you mind me collecting on Christmas?"

"Not at all," I purr.

"Good," he smiles, placing a light kiss on my lips.

CHAPTER ELEVEN

Our Date

Nelson

"Tell me something I haven't read about you on the internet or in a magazine," Talina chimes beside me while I navigate the Bentley Coupe around the countryside.

I hadn't planned to do more than listen to some music and go through paperwork today. After Talina came to talk to me in my office, I set to planning a romantic day at a little country cottage Detra talked me into buying.

The two-bedroom home is cozy and sits on a beautiful lot of land. I must admit, the lake on the back of the property drew me in. I've thought of building a second home on that end of the property.

When Talina's eyes sparkled with the prospects of a date, I thought of the quaint space. It's charm and its peace is something I think she will enjoy. I figured the drive would also give us time to get to know each other.

It's the reason I decided to drive and not have a car take us out. Although, now, I'm regretting the decision just a bit. I look over to see the bright, open, inquisitive look in Talina's eyes and I want to spill all of my secrets.

I've never allowed myself to be that vulnerable with anyone other than Detra, and believe me that's not by choice. Detra has been there through my worst moments. She's kept me from harming myself and others.

"What do you want to know?" I ask looking back at the road.

"What makes Nelson Fisher tick? You're so driven. Being here has shown me so much more of your vision. It's amazing! What drives you to be…," I chance a glance at her when her pause fills the car with silence. The awe I see in her eyes floors me. "Determined, I guess."

She finishes her sentence, when our eyes connect. I think her words over, before I answer. I guess I have become driven over the years. The question is, what has been the force behind that?

The words start to spill, before I can process them. "You," I surprise myself with the confession. "I used to want to get as far away from my past as I could get. At seventeen, Detra and I took off. We went our separate ways. I got a little apartment over a coffee shop. It was the only thing I could afford, but it was better than nothing.

"I worked at a printing press for two years. Detra would call here and there, but I never thought she would come back. Too much had changed.

"One day, she walked her tiny ass into the printing press, dressed in a fur and dripping in diamonds, yelling my name. When she spotted me, she said, 'Let's get the fuck out of here. You have a dream we need to build.'

"We walked out of there and never looked back. I built my company thinking I needed to prove myself. I had to prove them wrong. Prove the voices in my head wrong.

"Then one day, this brown eyed dove walked into my company. Everything changed, I stopped trying to prove myself. My company started to do better than it had ever done.

"I realized I had nothing to prove. Instead, my drive became wanting to see that dove spread her wings. I'd created a place where she could do that and I wanted to maintain that," I chance a glance over at her.

Talina sits staring at me with damp lashes and misty eyes. She leans over and kisses my cheek. I want to turn into the kiss, but I force myself to focus on the road.

I haven't driven this car that many times. The few times I have, the ride had been smooth. I don't know, since about thirty minutes into the ride, the car has seemed like it's pulling or something.

We're not to the cottage yet, but not that far out. I've been hoping it's just me, but I do intend to call a car out to pick us up for the return drive home.

"I like Detra. We bonded the night before we left. She wanted to stick around to make sure I was okay. I was embarrassed at first, but we had a good laugh and ended up spending the night talking while I packed for the trip," Talina says.

"Yeah, I guess I understand why she told me to give you a—," my words are cutoff by a loud sound from outside the car.

I tighten my hands on the steering wheel. The ground is wet beneath us, making it muddy and slick. I maneuver the car to keep us from slamming into a tree. I pump the breaks, but they don't stop the car. I try again, still no success.

"Shit," I mutter under my breath, trying to pump the breaks again.

I think fast and pull the emergency break. My heart is slamming against my ribs as we finally come to a stop. My jaw ticks as my mind spins.

I get the gut feeling this wasn't a coincidence or accident. Not wanting to alarm Talina, I swallow my anger.

I turn to make sure she's okay. Her knuckles are tight around the seatbelt strap. Her chest heaving, eyes wide. The fear I see on her face almost sends my rage into overdrive, but I fight it back.

"Are you okay?" I reach to brush her hair behind her ear.

She gives a jerky nod of her head. I reach to unfasten her seatbelt, pulling her into my embrace. I kiss the top of her head and wait for her body to relax.

I pull my phone out and curse when I see the lack of signal. I don't feel safe sitting out here. I've survived off of my instincts. In this moment, they're telling me to take Talina and get out of here.

"We can't stay here," I murmur into her hair when I feel her calm.

It's freezing out. It's Christmas. I doubt we'll be able to get a tow anytime soon. The cottage isn't that far. It's a good walk, but we can manage.

"What are we going to do? That was clearly more than a flat tire," Talina lifts her head to look up at me.

"We can walk it from here. I'll send someone for the car. We'll take what we need. Our bags aren't that heavy," I reassure her.

She licks her lips and nods. I climb from the car and circle it. My eyes narrow at the front left blown tire. I squat to look under the car. I can see fluid dripping onto the light snow on the ground, staining it yellow.

I grit my teeth and stand. I hear Detra's voice in the back of my head. She didn't think I should've made this trip to London without security. I've never been into having security or people fussing over me.

I keep security at the office for my workers, but I've yet to start to travel with a personal detail on a regular—much to Detra's disapproval. I fought my way through our old neighborhood. I think I can protect myself.

"That wasn't just a flat, was it," I hear Talina's voice come from over my shoulder.

"I'll know better once I have someone look at it," I reply.

"I'm not asking. I'm telling you," she says, causing me to turn to look at the concern on her face. "Who would want to hurt you?"

I blow out a long breath. The list is long enough. Talina just doesn't need to worry about that. Now that I have her to think of, I will be changing a lot about my life. She could've been hurt today. I would never have forgiven myself for that.

I reach to tug the collar of her coat tighter. "Come, we can talk at the cottage," I say, avoiding her question.

I open the trunk, retrieving both our overnight bags and the bag with the gift I bought for Talina. I decide to come back for the rest, once I have her safe in the cottage.

~*B*~

Talina

Nelson is silent during the walk to the cottage. I don't much mind as my own thoughts swirl while we barrel through the cold. Nelson refused to let me carry anything, allowing me to pull my coat tightly around me and hold it.

I'm so grateful for the snow boots I decided to wear for the trip. I truly think I'm going to freeze to death just as Nelson's voice vibrates through me with warmth. "We're here," he grumbles.

"Thank, God," I huff, seeing my breath puff out before me.

"I'll get a fire going when we get inside. You can take the master. Take a hot shower and change into something warm," Nelson says. I can hear the absences in his words.

A chill runs through me that has nothing to do with the cold outside. Someone tried to harm Nelson. I know cars. I used to hang with my dad in the garage on weekends, tinkering with his pride and joy. That was not just a blown-out tire back there.

Nelson knows it as well. His silence speaks volumes. We were enjoying our time together before the car nearly crashed. My queasy stomach makes me question if we'll be able to get back to that.

I'm grateful as we push our way into the cottage. It's gorgeous. Quaint and cozy, but decorated with such care and charm. I fall in love instantly.

Nelson drops our bags by the bedroom doors before moving to start a fire. His shoulders look so tense, I decide to follow his instructions and give him time to settle his mind. I hop in the shower and thank the stars for the hot water that warms my skin.

I'm so disappointed with this last turn of events. Nelson and I stayed up late talking last night. It wasn't about anything heavy. I'd been cautious after his question about Malcolm. I'd thought I'd get more time to pry today.

My heart sinks, when I think of how closed off Nelson became on the walk here. I noticed that's common with him, the ability to shut down. I'm not sure how I feel about that.

I want to call it childish, but Mya is the same way. When she doesn't want to deal, she avoids, shuts down, and withdraws. Honestly, I can do the same from time to time.

I get out of the shower and look around the spacious master bedroom. It's larger than I thought it would be, as is the en suite. The exposed beams and charming windowseat pull the space into the cozy feel of the rest of the cottage.

I look at the king-sized bed and think of yesterday morning in my room. I know Nelson and I said we'd take it slow, but I wouldn't mind finishing what we started. On the drive here, I was sort of hopeful that we'd share a room anyhow.

"Talina," I nearly jump out of my skin, dropping my towel to the floor.

I turn to find Nelson's hooded gaze on me. I look at Nelson, really look at him. He may not be traditionally handsome, but he has this sex appeal that's undeniable. His eyes are what arrest you, not just their hazel color, but those long, thick lashes and his piercing gaze.

When Nelson looks at you, he looks *at* you. His lips are another feature that seem to call out to me. I can't help remembering how they felt yesterday. My nipples pebble with the memory of how they felt sucking on them.

"I want to feed you and get you warm. Please, put that towel back around you, before we both starve and I become your sole source of heat," he says thickly.

"I have no problem with that. Truly, I don't," I breathe.

Nelson chuckles. "If my balls and toes weren't frozen I would pounce on you with no question. Since they are, I'm going to take that as a sign that we need to stick to taking things slow," he shakes his head.

I bend and pick up the towel. "Fine, suit yourself," I pout.

"I just wanted to check on you, before I jump in the shower," he says with a crooked smile. It's a nice smile, not perfect, but just about.

"I'm fine. I'll get dressed and see what we have to eat," I offer.

"Not a chance. I planned to cook for you. There's wine in the kitchen. Get a glass and make yourself comfortable in front of the fire," he says, before turning for the hall bath.

I sigh and get dressed. I put on a beige off the shoulder, sweater dress that stops just above my knees. It complements my curves in all the right ways. After a bit of a debate with myself, I put on a thong and a pair of fishnet stockings. I know I'm not playing fair, but a sister has needs.

I pull my hair up into a ponytail and sashay my butt into the kitchen for that glass of wine. I'm sitting comfortably in front of the fire when Nelson returns dressed in slacks and a sweater that hugs his arms and torso in a way that shows off his muscled physique.

The sweater is rolled up to his elbows and his feet are bare. I catch myself just before I lick my lips. I'm not the only one not playing fair.

"Are you in the mood for Christmas carols?" he asks, moving to a panel that reveals an entertainment unit.

"Sure, why not," I say huskily and want to kick myself.

I clear my throat and turn back to watch the fire. I still haven't figured out what it is about this man that just does something to me.

Music fills the room, but I can still hear Nelson moving in the kitchen. The music lulls me into a peaceful trance. It doesn't take long before the cottage is filled with delicious aromas. My stomach starts to grumble a little, as my mouth waters. I hope it tastes as good as it smells.

I take my empty wine glass to fill it again. Making sure to put a little extra sway in my hips. I feel his eyes on me as I try not to look in his direction.

"Where'd you learn to cook," I ask, as I pour my second glass of wine.

"Detra's mother loved to cook?" Nelson replies.

I smile and look over at him. My mouth drops. The food smells delicious, but Nelson looks a hot sweaty mess. His hair is pasted to his forehead, his cheeks are red.

All this time, I thought he had it covered in here. I'd been sipping my wine and relaxing by the fire. I thought he had this. The kitchen looks a mess right along with him.

"Oh, my God, Nelson, do you know what you're doing?" I gasp.

He frowns and looks up at me. "It looks worse than it is. It'll be fine," he murmurs.

I throw my head back and laugh. "If you don't get out of this kitchen," I chuckle.

"No, I want to do this. I promise you it may not look good, but it will taste great," he says, with a blush and boyish smile.

I see the plea in his eyes and my heart jerks in my chest. I push my sleeves up and look around at the mess. I won't takeover, but I'll help to clean up some of this.

"It better be good," I playfully mumble and bump him with my hip.

He wraps his arm around me, placing his hand on my waist. "It will be great," he says against my temple, then places a kiss there.

My belly flips and my scalp tingles. I'm in so much damn trouble when it comes to this man. I look up into his eyes and smile at the wrinkles around his eyes, as they smile back at me.

"Tell me something else about you," I say, while moving to wash the dishes.

"There's not much to tell. I grew up rough. I was the white kid in the neighborhood. I got my ass beat, until I got tired of it and started to fight back.

"Everyone thought I'd be easy to pick on, until I wasn't anymore. After a while, they either tried to jump me or just left me alone. Detra and her siblings helped a lot. When we became friends, they had my back.

"I hated my childhood," he says, with so much loathing dripping from the words.

"How about high school? No special girlfriend or anything," I turn to say and smile.

Only, the icy look that covers his face, makes me wish I hadn't said a word. His jaw works, his fist clenches at his side. I can see I've struck a big nerve.

"There was a girl, but that didn't turn out so well," he finally replies.

"I don't think I found myself until freshman year in college," I say with a smile, trying to change the subject. "Forget about dating. I was so socially awkward."

Nelson looks at me and lifts a brow. "I have a hard time believing that. You make everyone in the office feel at ease," he murmurs.

"Yeah, now," I give a short laugh. "In high school, I always said what I thought. I'm guessing I was a little too honest for the other adolescent minds."

"I think that's one of the things I like about you. You're not afraid to say what's on your mind. It gives the clients a sense of security and the feeling that you know what you're doing with their interests," he muses.

I watch him make faces at the pot he's stirring. I roll my lips, trying not to laugh at him. His eyes flash up to mine and a deep blush takes over his cheeks. It's so endearing.

"I'm going to be honest with you now. I'm afraid to eat that," I burst out with the laughter I've been holding.

"Come here," he waves me over.

I purse my lips and look at him cautiously. I'm hesitant to move near him at first, looking around at the mess and the pot he is stirring. When I look into his hopeful hazel orbs, I cave.

I move forward and stop before him. Nelson places a hand on my hip and tugs me into his side, lifting the spoon to my lips. I lean forward and give the spoon a tentative lick.

The taste bursts on my tongue in a delicious explosion of flavors. I go back in to wrap my lips around the spoon for more. It's so good.

I cover my mouth and moan. "Wow, that's amazing," I say, nodding my head.

I guess you can't judge a book by its cover. As if to prove my point, Nelson drops the spoon on the counter and cups the side of my face. His lips are on mine faster than I can blink.

This man's kisses are drugging. It's like he's eating my face, but not in a sloppy teenage boy way. It's controlled, demanding, and all-consuming. I reach to lock my fingers in his hair, pulling a deep groan from his throat.

Much too quickly for my liking, Nelson pulls away. I lean into the counter on my unsteady legs, trying to catch my breath. Nelson licks his full bottom lip, as his eyes roll over my body.

"We'll be able to eat in a few," is all he says, turning his attention back to the pots before him.

I decide to get out of his way and go set the small table by the window. It's an oak round kitchenette set that speaks to the allure of the cottage. The rich blue flowers in the center of the table tie in with the blue throws and pillows from the living room area.

I love the combinations of blues, soft greys, and beiges. It almost has a beachy cottage feel. I get the feeling Detra was the one that had a hand in this décor.

I'm surprised by the ping of jealousy I feel. Nelson has mentioned her as a part of his life several times. She must know so much about him. Detra is a beautiful woman, I can't help wondering if they were ever involved romantically.

Which totally shocks me, I've never been the jealous type. My thoughts start to circle a million things, from my attraction to Nelson, his relationship with Detra, the near car accident, and what this date truly means to our relationship. I'm placing the last glass on the table when I feel Nelson walk up behind me.

"I'm glad you're here," he says into my ear, wrapping his arms around my waist.

I turn in his embrace and look up at him. "I am too. You're full of surprises, Nelson. I'm interested to find out more," I beam up at him.

His eyes grow dark. "Be careful what you ask for," he purrs, giving my backside a little squeeze.

I swallow back my reply. I don't want to beg for it and I don't want to come off needy. I've already thrown out there that I'm interested.

Nelson searches my eyes, taking on a little look of disappointment, when I don't reply. I bite my lip, confused by the sudden change in his expression. Lord, this man is giving me whiplash.

I go to make the reply I'd held back, but Nelson pecks my forehead and turns to get our food. I take a seat at the table. When he places a plate before me, I roll my lips again.

"Smells delicious," I compliment.

"It's one of my favorites," he says, with the cutest shy smile.

My heart flips over. Suddenly, I want to dive into this plate and finish every morsel. The aromas of garlic bread, fresh tomato sauce, and basil fill my lungs.

"Fresh marinara sauce over sausage and Orzo. Nice," I nod.

I fork a bite and pop it into my mouth. Oh, my God. If I thought the little taste I had before was divine. This is just amazing. The pasta is cooked to perfection.

"Everyone always says I'm like a tornado in the kitchen, but I'm the perfect storm in your mouth," Nelson chuckles.

I nearly choke at the visual that pops in my head. I reach for my glass of wine, as my eyes water. You would think I was a slut.

Yes, I can be a freak in the bedroom. At least, I think I am, but I've never been openly aggressive or provoking. Nelson seems to bring that side out.

His eyes widen. "Are you okay? Is it too spicy?" he asks.

I shake my head. "No, it's not the food," I cover my forehead, trying to collect my thoughts.

A few beats pass and I hear Nelson's rumbling laugh. "That did come out bad, didn't it?" he laughs out.

"Yeah, sort of," I feel myself blush.

"I promise. This once, that was not my intention," he says, voice laced with amusement.

I drop my hands into my lap. "I just need to say something," I say softly. "What happened yesterday and what I said earlier are so unlike me. I've never had sex outside a relationship and mostly well into the relationship. I just don't want to give you the wrong idea about me."

"Then, I guess it's a very good thing we're in a relationship," Nelson gives me a heated smile. "I'll make a deal with you. We'll both stop overthinking this, before we mess things up."

"Deal," I chirp.

"Let's finish our meal so I can give you your Christmas present," he says lightly.

"Sounds good," I reply, wanting nothing more than to devour the rest of the dish before me. Well, the food and the man.

CHAPTER TWELVE

Merry Christmas

Nelson

Talina has done more than enough to distract me from my thoughts of my car being tampered with. That dress alone has my mind in a million places it shouldn't be. I keep telling myself the wait will be worth it, but in the back of my mind, I feel like I've waited forever already.

When she didn't deny or try to refute us being in a relationship, I thought my chest would burst. I feel seventeen all over again. Only this time, my mother isn't in the picture to ruin this for me.

I couldn't bring myself to tell Talina of the humiliation I felt so many years ago. I was grateful to her when she changed the subject. Those events shaped so much about who I am, as a man now.

It shaped the gift I decided to give Talina for Christmas. Now that it's time to give it to her, I'm nervous. It feels like it's not enough. I should've gone with something more...I don't know.

She wasn't mine at the time I put it all together, not officially. My chest tightens with the thought of disappointing her. I'll have to go out and get her something more when we return to London.

"The wrapping is so pretty. I don't want to open it," she says, as her eyes sparkle.

I hate myself for getting her something so simple. I don't think I can bear to watch the disappointment that will appear on her face. I'm a fucking millionaire. What was I thinking?

"You don't have to open it. You can wait until we go back," I rush out.

"Nope, I'm too excited," she looks up at me, with those bright eyes and I want to hurl.

Talina tugs the ribbon on the box free. I watch her excitement, as she lifts the lid and sets it aside. She squeals a bit, as she reaches into the box.

"M & M's," she holds the glass jar, filled with the chocolate candies to her chest. I had them customized with her name on them. "These are my favorite!"

"I know. You keep a bag of them stashed in your desk for emergencies," I grin.

She tilts her head at me. "I'm always amazed at the things you know about me," she says sweetly.

I feel my cheeks blush, sure that they're flaming red. Talina leans forward to place a kiss on my cheek, before returning her attention to the gift box. She reaches in and pulls out the blue and grey scarf and her laughter fills the room.

"I thought I told you no one should spend three hundred dollars on one damn scarf." She gives me a pointed look.

"I thought I told you, it looked amazing on you. I'll spoil my woman if I want to," I mutter back, returning her pointed look.

I hadn't known she would be mine, when I bought the scarf. I'd gone back that day we'd gone shopping and purchased it. It truly did look exquisite on her. It brings out her chocolate complexion and the warmth in her brown eyes.

"Mm-um," she makes the small sound, but I see the glow in her cheeks, before she dips her head and digs back into the box.

Talina slowly lifts the book from inside the box. It's the one that her father quoted on the last night they talk to each other. I wanted her to have it.

I clench my fists at my sides. There's nothing else in the box. This is my gift. No expensive jewelry, no keys to an expensive car. I don't do gifts that will make me feel used. I refuse to buy love.

I wait for her to realize that's all I got her. I hold my breath, waiting for the disappointment, already knowing I plan to promise her something more. Surprisingly, I do want to spoil her.

Only, when she lifts her gaze to me, it's not disappointment I see in her eyes. It's tears that fill her beautiful orbs. She places the book aside and crawls over into my lap. We've been sitting in front of the fire, while Talina shared stories of Christmas time with her family.

She cups the sides of my face, staring into my eyes. "Thank you," her voice comes out shakily. Her eyes search mine some more. "That was one of the most thoughtful gifts anyone has ever given me."

Her lips press softly to mine once, then again. I grasp her waist, as she moves to deepen the kiss. At that point I take over, devouring her sweet mouth.

I grow so hard, I think I might rip through my pants. When Talina starts to rock her hips into me, I release a long hiss. I grasp her hips to still her movements.

Placing my head to her chin, I try to rein in my sanity. We talked about taking it slow. We keep this up, slow is the last thing I'll be doing.

"Baby, I have but so much self-control," I say.

"Good, so it won't take much more to break you," she pants.

I look up into her eyes. She has the smile of a temptress on her lips. I'd hoped she'd make one of her smart offers earlier, before dinner. After trying to tug out my release in the shower, I wanted her more, instead of less.

I reach to wrap her ponytail around my hand, giving it a gentle tug. I look over her heart shaped face. I've never seen a woman more beautiful.

"Say the word, Talina. I'll break you and put you back together again," I reply.

"*Fuck*, please," she whimpers. "Saying shit like that. Hell, yes."

I chuckle, but tug her face to mine to take her lush mouth. Forget slow, I know what I want and I want it now. With my free hand, I pull her dress up over her waist. I've been eyeing her fishnet covered legs all day, wanting to see them wrapped around me.

Reaching between us, I tear at the crotch, creating a hole right in the center. When I find her core, I find it hot, slick, and ready. The heat coming off of her is scorching.

Slipping her thong to the side, I caress her petals and feel them weep on my fingertips. I drag my lips from hers, kissing my way down her neck to her exposed shoulder. Her skin is so soft, it's almost unreal.

"That's it, baby," I murmur in her ear, when she starts to fuck my fingers.

I love how responsive she is to me. Her hands steady her on my shoulders, as she rocks against my digits. I can feel her tight pussy tightening with her oncoming release.

She tries to pull back, shaking her head. I smile, knowing it's a powerful one. I release her hair, to tug down the front of her dress, exposing her full breasts inside a lacy strapless bra.

I yank the right cup down, freeing the heavy mound from its support. I groan, when her plump flesh bounces free, like an offering of ripe fruit. Dipping my head, I receive the offering, as if it's my last.

"Nelson," she cries out, still trying to tug away from my fingers working her drenched heat.

I won't let her get away. This is what she wanted, this is what we both wanted. "Take it," I hiss against her nipple. "Stop running."

"Ugh, I'm coming. It's too much," she gasps.

"It's nothing, Honey. I haven't even started," I croon.

~B~

Talina

What? He hasn't started? My brain short circuits and I come screaming. *From just his hand? This is unreal.* I sag against his shoulder.

Never, ever has a man touched me like that. Oh, I've had some pussy killers in my life. My exes were all skilled in their own ways, but none have set my body on fire like Nelson has with a simple touch and just as simple words.

Even now, his gentle strokes against the small of my back, have my body humming with need, as if I didn't just blow a blood vessel with that climax. I sigh, when I feel him placing soft kisses on my head.

His hands move, pulling my dress up and over my head. I move sluggishly to allow him to do so. I brace myself on his shoulders again, while watching him stare at my breasts and remove my bra.

His hand moves between us. I gasp, when he rips my thong right from between my legs, through the gaping hole in my tights. Nelson eases me back, until I meet with the soft rug beneath me. He reaches a hand up to push my gifts and the box out of our way.

I watch the top of his head, as he kisses his way down my center. I sigh and arch off the floor, when he reaches my sweet spot on my hip. Taking notice of my reaction, he pauses there, swirling his tongue against my skin.

I try to squirm away, but he pins me in place and keeps on with his assault. I reach to anchor myself with my hands in his hair, tugging tightly. I buck hard, when I feel his teeth sink into my flesh, causing me to gush and spasm below.

"I need to taste you," he purrs.

He lifts my legs over his shoulders, tearing the hole in my stockings wider for his own access. I release his hair lifting to my elbows, looking down at him. I moan loudly, while I watch him become enthralled in eating my core.

I've never seen a man so dedicated to eating pussy. It feels so good, but the sight...Lord, the sight of him worshiping my flower is something awe inspiring. He nips and tugs at my clit, his long lashes lifting, as he looks up at me.

The look in his eyes is so sexy. Like he's dying for more. It slams into me so hard, I fall back against the rug beneath me. I push my fingers into the front of my own hair. My stomach clenches and my thighs shake.

He sucks on my clit to sooth it and I come once again. I do believe this man has just sucked my soul out through my pussy. Maybe even a bit of my brain.

I hear more than see him unfasten his slacks. I fight to clear the fog from my head. The music in the background helps. It changed to R&B a while ago.

Beyoncé's, *Rocket,* fills the room, I want to do just what she purrs out. I lift, as Nelson pulls his sweater over his head. I place my hands on his waist and run them up his smooth skin, watching his muscle flex. I give a gentle push and he falls back onto his ass, against the couch behind him.

I look down and my mouth waters, he's so much bigger than I imagined. Thick and long, his pale flesh reaches up, as if calling to me. It pulses as if beckoning me forward. Placing my hands on his shoulders, I straddle his lap.

I rub my slickness over him, wetting the head. I smile, when he groans and grasps a hold of my globes. I reach between us to grip him in my palm. I stroke him, once, twice, but I don't get in the third pass.

Nelson grabs my hand and thrusts forward into my waiting folds. My head falls back and my eyes roll, as I slide down onto him. He feels so good. My breath swooshes past my lips.

"This pussy is mine now," he growls.

I lift my head and look him in the eyes. If it were possible for a man's eyes to be on fire, I would swear I'm staring right into flames. His hips rock up into me, as I rock and swirl mine.

He's so big. I'm trying my best to handle him and give back as much as I can. I have to breathe through my nose, as he stretches me wide.

"Damn, baby," I whisper.

He slaps my ass, causing my back to arch, pushing my breasts into his face. I feel my pussy spasm with another orgasm. I can't believe I've come so fast again.

Nelson squeezes my ass in his hands and guides me, as I try to slowdown to ride the wave out. He's having none of that. He pounds up into me, dipping his head, seeking out my breast.

When his lips wrap my nipple, my orgasm ripples into multiples. My mouth falls open on a silent scream. *This motherfucker! Oh, shit! Yes, Nelson, do that shit!*

I have to scream the words in my head because my voice has left my body. I crumble in his hands. He's wrecking my walls. Why in the world did I think I should play with this man?

My nipple pops free from his lips. "That's it, baby. Come all over that cock. You feel that, it's all yours," he croons.

I shiver, at the look in his eyes. I cup his face and take his lips. He takes over the kiss, as usual. I'm on my back before I know it. Nelson shifts over me, breaking the kiss, he lifts my legs to his shoulders.

I didn't think it could get any better, but the feel of him rocking into me slowly, while gyrating his hips, has a keening sound spilling from my lips. My back arches off the floor.

"*Fuck*," Nelson growls and begins to pump harder.

"Oh, shit, I wasn't ready for this," I cry out, or at least, I think that comes from my lips.

I come again, but he pushes right through it. I tighten my walls around him. I need this man to come and give my ass a break, but at the same time, I don't ever want it to stop.

He grasps my ankles, shifting my legs to one shoulder and tilting my hips. My eyes roll and I grip a hold of the rug. "Nelson," I scream.

"Yes, baby?" he grunts.

His fingers run up my thighs, over my fishnet covered legs. The sensation spikes all the others, taking over my body. I feel like he's stirring my soul with his thick dick that's rubbing every inch of my insides and robbing me of every piece of my sanity.

I don't even know how I'm managing to rock back against him. It's a greedy, mindless gesture at this point. Nelson groans, reaching to squeeze my left breast. My eyes flutter as I feel like my soul is leaving my body.

My heart pounds in my chest. His thrusts are hard and controlled, as if his aim has a target right on the inside of me. A target he knows will shatter me into a million pieces.

It floats through my mind that I want to give this man babies. Shit, I'll lie naked tied to his bed, if he asked me to. Nelson is lethal. Every move has a purpose, to drive me insane.

I've lost track of my orgasms. I've also given up on trying to pull one from him. Nelson is in total control here. He'll come when he's ready.

I think he's reached his peak, when he pulls from my body. Oh, nope, so wrong. He swiftly shifts my body so I'm on all fours. His hand wraps around my ponytail again. He bends over my back kissing my ear. Slowly he enters me from behind.

I whimper and claw at the rug. My mouth falls open. I swear the man is trying to come through my back. My greedy pussy gushes with glee, rippling around him.

"You feel so good," he hisses in my ear. "Better than I ever dreamed. Come for me again. Stop fighting it."

"I can't," I whimper.

He reaches between my legs for my clit and starts to strum it. "See, yes, you can. Again," he growls.

"Nelson, fuck, Nelson," I scream, my throat raw.

"That's my name, baby. Call it all you want, I'm not stopping until I destroy this pussy," he grunts.

"Seriously," I whimper.

It was destroyed ten minutes ago. He's just showing off now. I turn my head to look back at him and frown, but that frown turns into something else, as I see the look on his face.

His eyes are filled with desire, his bottom lip is sucked into his mouth, as he bites down just above his chin. His brows are drawn together. His cheeks are flushed, as sweat drips from his face.

He looks like he's in the greatest moment of bliss he's ever had in his life. I want that for him. I'll hold on a little longer to give that to him.

His features softens just a bit, his eyes searching my face. He leans forward and takes my lips in a deep kiss, slowing his thrusts. If a kiss could speak, his says a million words.

You're going to fall for him, hard. The words ring in my head, but they're a lie. I know they are because I think I already have. There is no future tense.

My mind floats to his gift. It may be something so small to someone else, but the thought behind it all means the world to me. The thought alone causes me to open my heart.

Nelson nips my lower lip. "Come with me, Beautiful," he gasps.

I feel the moment he spills inside of me. I gasp and explode at the same time. A flood of emotions hit me and confusion sets in.

What the fuck just happened?

CHAPTER THIRTEEN

His World

Talina

I wake in the master bedroom alone, which is odd. I fell asleep in Nelson's arms last night, after he rocked me to the edge of sanity for the final time. I'm still thinking about my life.

We've been in this cottage for four days now. We were only supposed to stay the one night originally. One night turned into another and then another. I haven't come up for air long enough to care.

I sit up, pulling my knees into my chest, wrapping my arms around them. I wince as I feel the soreness between my legs. A little smile lifts my lips. I thought I knew great sex. Nelson masters my body in a way I can't even explain.

My smile falls as I seriously think about that. It sounds crazy, but I don't know if I can handle a man that throws it down this good. I'm terrified of Nelson. I could lose all my good sense to him.

Shit, I almost told him I love him more than once over the last few days. Yes, I know I have feelings for him. Yup, the kind that start to develop into love.

Shut the fuck up, Talina. You are in love with that man.

I sigh and place my head on top of my knees. Yup, I fear him because I am in love with him. Before I fell asleep last night, my mind raced with all of the kind things I can remember Nelson saying and doing for me.

My grandmother used to tell me and Mya to beware of the men you fall fast and hard for. They're the ones that walk away with your heart. I think of the kindness I see in Nelson's eyes when he allows his shield to come down. I want to believe he would never walk away and leave me hurting.

"Merry Christmas," my head pops up, as the words are sung into the room.

I don't have time to pull the sheet up over me, before Detra jumps her ass onto the bed. My eyes round and I pull my knees in closer, snatching at the sheets. She rolls onto her back and makes herself comfortable.

"Really," Nelson says dryly, from the doorway.

"What?" Detra shrugs. "Why don't you go make us some coffee?"

"Christmas was four days ago and Talina doesn't drink coffee," he mutters.

I can't help smiling at yet another thing he knows about me. Detra just makes herself at home beside me. I look down at her and lift a brow.

"Well, I wasn't here four days ago. Would have been here sooner," Detra pulls a frown.

"You could at least let her get dressed," Nelson sighs.

"Coffee," she growls at him.

"Spoiled fucking brat," Nelson mumbles and leaves the room.

"Love you too," she sings after him.

She then turns to me with a straight face. I tug the sheet up a little more. Detra doesn't seem to care that I'm butt ass naked beneath the covers.

Detra reaches in her mouth and pulls out a razor blade. I look at her like she's crazy and coil for a fight, tugging the sheet around me and tucking it into place. I'm no punk and I don't know what this little crazy woman is up to.

"You don't have to worry. Just listen closely to what I'm about to say," Detra says, shifting to look at me, as she rolls the blade through her fingers.

"Nelson is like a brother to me. We grew up rough, I learned to place polish on two tarnished people and now we glow to the world. We weren't always who you see now.

"I've watched Nelson get his ass beat just for being the only white boy around. I've watched people he loved treat him like shit and make him feel like it too. I've also watched it all make him into the man he is today.

"Me and my family, blood and those I've adopted over the years, it's our job to look out for Nelson. The business he has built takes care of a lot of people. People that love and respect him.

"Whoever played with his car. They're going to pay for that. Trust me," she places the blade back into her mouth.

"I'm more than what meets the eye. You see what I want you to see. What I want *you* to see, Talina, is that you are the most important person in the world to Nelson.

"Eventually, if someone wants to harm him, they will come for him through you. I'm here to keep that from happening. We play for the same team, Team Nelson. Don't let anyone tell you different." She holds up a hand, when I go to interrupt. Her eyes get sad.

"It's happened before. Before I could protect him. Some of the most important people in his life used his love to hurt him deeply. I don't think you will hurt him, but I have a feeling others will try to use you to," Detra says.

"Maybe it's better if I walk away now," I say to myself, more than her.

Detra throws her head back and laughs. "Oh, I know that look. He fucked your brains out and scrambled what's left up there." She bursts out, shaking her head. "They either run or come back begging for more."

I reach over to push at her arm. "Shut up," I pout.

"He wouldn't let you go now, even if you tried," Detra says, with a rueful smile.

"Who would tamper with his car?" I ask, going back to one of the things that has been plaguing me for days.

"I have a few ideas. I'll know more when my boys are done with the car," Detra shrugs.

I blow out a breath and rub my temples. I try to soak it all in. Dating Nelson will be different for me for so many reasons. I've never dated a millionaire before. Nor have I dated a white guy. That part doesn't bother me, though.

"You love him. I can see it," Detra breaks through my thoughts. "Don't overthink the rest."

I smile and look at her. "Can you love someone so fast?" I don't know if I'm asking her or myself.

Detra shrugs. "You two have had this thing for longer than you both realize. The lightbulb may have just turned on for you, but it has been there for a while."

I think over her words and can't really deny them. "I do love him. That shit scares the fuck out of me," I say softly.

Just as the words spill out, Nelson enters the room carrying two mugs. He hands one to Detra, but his eyes remain on me. He skirts the bed, coming to my side, placing the mug on the side table.

His hand goes into the mess that is my hair. He tugs my head back and captures my lips hard. I reach to cling to his shoulders.

"I'll be in the guestroom," Detra sings, as she's forgotten.

I hear the door close behind her. Nelson breaks the kiss and looks me in my eyes. "I love you," he says the words with such caution in them.

His words almost sound like a plea not to hurt him. I cup his face, watching as he reveals a side of him I know in my heart he keeps hidden from others. I kiss his lips.

"I love you too," I say with a smile.

CHAPTER FOURTEEN

My Valentine

Talina

The last eight weeks have been a whirlwind. I haven't smiled so much in…I don't know how long. I thought working with Nelson would become awkward, but things have only gotten better.

We're at the point of finishing each other's sentences. Nelson anticipates me in so many ways. We have become one well-oiled machine.

All of my fears have melted with each day. Nelson still shatters me to bits on a nightly basis, but he's there to hold me after, over and over again. Today is the first day I've felt out of sorts and it's not because of our relationship.

Valentine's day was special in my household growing up. My dad made my mom feel like a queen and me and my sister got to be princesses. My first dozen red roses came from my dad.

Over the years, I watched him give my mother countless roses and shower her in gifts of love, joy, and laughter. Their love was true love. I've always thought I'd have to settle for something less than that.

Nelson had an important meeting this morning, but he insisted that I take the day off. I woke to a trail of rose petals leading into the bathroom. A warm bath and bottle of wine waiting for me.

I broke down in tears. Nelson doesn't know how much the simple things mean to me. The gesture is something my mother would have smiled all day about. Something I would have overheard her telling her sisters about.

God, my Mom and Dad loved each other. It was something we all felt. Finding Nelson's note to me, along with a new jar of M & M's and a diamond bracelet, gave me hope that I've finally found that same kind of love.

It's been a melancholy type of day, so bittersweet. I don't have Detra here to keep me laughing. She had to return to the States a few weeks ago. I have to say, I miss her.

I thought about calling Mya, but I don't want to bring her down. Not after she called this morning, squealing about the text she sent me. She couldn't even wait long enough for me to receive it and open it on my own. My heart nearly burst through my chest to see the amazing ring Jin placed on her finger.

I'm so happy for them. Mom and Dad would be so proud of her. Jin has been in love with my sister for as long as they've known each other.

I swipe at a tear and give a watery smile as the song on my phone starts to play from the beginning again. Ella belts out, *My Funny Valentine*. I can't remember a Valentine's day when this didn't play in my home.

I feel Nelson's arms go around my waist as I stand at the window in the sitting room. I close my eyes and breathe him in. His scent feels like home to me now.

"Are you trying to tell me something?" he says, his words sounding a little harsh.

I turn to look up at him. His words were hard, but I see nothing but love in his eyes. I cup his face and lift on my toes to kiss his lips.

"My father was a very handsome man, but he would always tell my mom how he somehow got lucky to have her," I smile at the memory, as more tears fill my eyes. "Every Valentine's day, he'd play this song, teasing as he danced Mom around the living room."

Nelson's eyes soften. He brushes away my tears and kisses my lips. He begins to sway me in his arms.

"I'm glad you have fond memories of it. Mine are very different."

I knit my brows. "How so?"

At first, I don't think he's going to respond. His jaw works and his eyes go distant. I'm used to him avoiding a topic when he gets like this.

I sort of wish this was one of those times as his words proceed to shatter my heart. I've wondered so many times in the last few months where Nelson goes in his head. I've wondered about the darkness he and Detra have hinted at.

I never thought I would find out the answer like this. I never thought this ugliness would be the response. I think I fall in love with the soul of the man that stands before me, as he unravels his truth.

"My mother used every opportunity she had to make me feel like shit. I've been called ugly by her more times than I can count. She was never kind to me.

"I can still hear her cackling, while this song played. She'd tease me with it, and not in a good way. She'd laugh when I'd come home and didn't get a Valentine's day card from anyone.

"When I was seventeen there was this girl. I had such a big crush on her. We'd been friends, or at least I thought we were.

"I thought she was my girlfriend. I'd gotten up the nerve to ask her out and she said yes. We were together for a few months. Then, on Valentine's day, at the dance in front of everyone, this song came on.

"My heart stopped the moment I heard it. I looked around and in the middle of the school gym, was my girlfriend kissing someone else. When I went to walk out of the gym, my mother was there, smoking a cigarette with a smug grin on her face.

"I didn't know my mother was paying her to lead me on. It wasn't even much, but back then we all needed something. It was enough to betray me.

"That woman wanted to break me. My father made her promises he never kept and I had to pay for them. She ripped me apart until the day I left her behind," Nelson's last words echo with so much pain.

"I'm so sorry," I whisper, wrapping my arms around his waist. "I wish I could take all of that away."

He looks into my eyes and strokes my wet cheek. "You have," he says with a weak smile.

"I love you," I reassure him.

"Do you think you can see yourself with me?" Nelson asks sincerely. The worry in his eyes baffles me. I love him so much. "I mean, in a forever way."

I push his hair off his forehead. "I've been looking for you all my life, Nelson. Since I was a little girl, I've wanted what I saw my father give my mother. A love that touched not only their souls, but the souls of everyone around them and everyone that watched them.

"You know, that forever love. The kind that changes everything. That love that draws you together, no matter what. The type of love that can conquer anything. I think I have that now. With you. So I'm not going anywhere. You're stuck with me." I smile into those expressive hazel eyes.

Nelson licks his lips and nods. He blows out a breath. "I was hoping you would say that," he says and drops to one knee. He gives me a broad smile. "Keep breathing, Ta."

"Nelson," I gasp and clench my t-shirt over my belly.

He pulls a box from inside his suit jacket. "I've been shopping for the right one for weeks. It had to be perfect, just like you. When you called me all excited about your sister, I wanted to tell you then," Nelson draws in a breath and blows it out.

"I have a hard time trusting people. I've had more failed relationships than I care to count, but all of that has taught me to cherish when I have something special. You, Talina are the most precious part of my life.

"I want to spend the rest of my life with you. I want to grow old with you and dance around our living room every year to our song to remember this year, over and over again. Will you be my Valentine? Will you be my wife? Will you marry me?"

"Yes, yes, and yes," I squeal and throw myself at him.

Nelson catches me, but my momentum is too strong. I knock him over and he cracks his head on the floor. I gasp and Nelson groans, reaching for the back of his head.

"Are you okay? I'm so sorry," I rush out.

"I'm fine," he chuckles.

"I'm so, so sorry," I repeat, dropping kisses all over his face. "I'm sorry."

We look at each other and burst into laughter. Nelson wraps his arms around me and buries his face into my hair. I wrap my arms around his neck and absorb all the love he fills me with.

~*B*~

Nelson

I was thrown back in time when I heard that song. I almost turned to leave. Only, there was something in the way Talina had been standing at the window.

Taking her in brought me back to the present, back to the woman I've been sharing my life with for the last two months. I knew then that it was time to share my past with her. Talina has healed me with each day. I have nothing I want to keep from her.

I'm glad I didn't walk away. Talina is finally mine forever. I'm going to make her my wife. We're going to share a lifetime of the love she spoke so passionately about.

"I love you so much," I say, against her breast.

Once she said yes, I wasted no time tossing her over my shoulder and carrying her up to our bedroom. Well, I did so after she flung herself at me, knocking me to the floor, where I cracked my head. My life is always filled with laughter with Talina around.

However, this moment will be filled by many sounds, just not laughter. I drag my tongue from one nipple over to the other. I love the taste of her chocolate skin on my tongue.

I get ready to pull her peak into my mouth, but Talina has other ideas. She catches me off guard, as she pushes me onto my back. She moves her small frame to rest between my legs.

My lips part, as her intention hits me. She pulls me into her mouth, swirling her tongue around the crown. I groan and push my head back into the pillow. I suck in a breath, as she works her head up and down.

"Baby," I groan and rock my hips up.

The slurping sound that greets my ears sets my blood on fire. My toes curl as she plants her palms on my thighs. Her fingernails dig into my skin, and my hands shoot into her hair.

"Talina," I hiss. "Damn, baby."

"Mmm," she hums and it's the last straw, I gently peel her off.

I cup my hands under her arms and drag her up my body. I roll until she's beneath me. My thighs nudge her legs apart.

When I slide inside her, I grasp the sheets beside her head. This will never get old, she's always so snug. I shift my leg up further, tilting her hips up and sliding my knees beneath her. I want to go deeper than deep.

I want to feel every inch of my woman. I set a slow pace, making love to her, not fucking. Chest to chest, heart to heart, I feel her soul connect with mine. I drink from her lips, taking her cries for my own air. They give me a new life, as I slide back and forth, over and over and over.

Our love making is the only sound that matters, as we call for each other and breathe for one another. She is everything I was made to love. Feeling her soak my hard cock is like a prize in itself.

"I love you with everything I am," I groan in her ear.

"I love you too, Nelson," she pants. "Please, I need more."

I grin, knowing just what she needs. I lift to sit back on my haunches. Scooping my hands beneath her, I lift her up so that we're chest to chest again. I coax her legs around my back, then guide her up and down on my length.

Her head falls back, I lean in to lick her neck before I suck her flesh into my mouth. I kiss my way down to her breast, kissing the mound before using my tongue to seek out her tight peak. I suck her sensitive trigger into my mouth, finding the sensitive skin on her hips with my hands at the same time.

I tease her skin with my fingers, while taunting her breast with my mouth. Her cries tell me all I need to know. The rocking and rolling of her hips takes me to the edge of my restraint.

My fingers dig into her hips, biting into her flesh. "Yes, Nelson, yes, baby," she purrs.

This woman. She had me from the beginning. I would give her the world, yet she never asks for more than my love. I can do that.

~B~

Talina

If this is what I have to look forward to as Nelson's wife, I want to get married tonight. I didn't think he could take my body any higher. Boy, was I wrong.

My breast pops free from his mouth. How is watching his saliva connect from his lip to my nipple so sexy? I feel like every nerve in my body is soaring. How does one ooze sexy, during the act of sex? Nelson has changed everything I ever thought about sex.

"Baby, I'm coming," I breathe.

"Then, come, I'm here to catch you. Fall as hard as you need to," he says and that's all it takes.

I fall and I fall hard, but it doesn't hurt because he's there to bring me down gently. I know in my heart this will always be the way it is. Nelson will catch me every single time and I love him for it.

ACKNOWLEDGMENTS

I needed this book for me. I needed something light and fun to break state from all of the heavy stuff I'm writing. I love these two. I almost didn't give them life, but they wouldn't leave me alone. I know for a fact they will be back.

Thank you for coming on another journey with me. There is so much going on and I'm hoping to continue to bring you lots of words this year. I think we will all be happy with the turnout. I hope this brought you some Valentines love, laughter, and heat.

Once again, thank you to my husband. He listens to me talk to myself about these books, but most of all he understands that I write what comes to me and what I need to write. He doesn't judge me or try to change me, while the world tries to influence God's design.

As for God's design. I do this by His grace. This is what I know I must never forget. Faith is not easy to have, but when you have it, everything else is easy. You can watch an anointing, but you can't duplicate it. That's God's job and he never makes two of the same. I love the blessing that's uniquely me. I thank God for that and will continue in the Blue print.

Eyes open he's coming very soon.
Braxton, do you think they're ready?

ABOUT THE AUTHOR

Blue Saffire, award-winning, bestselling author of over thirty contemporary romance novels and novellas,—writes with the intention to touch the heart and the mind. Blue hooks, weaves, and loops multiple series, keeping you engaged in her worlds. Every word is meant to have a lasting touch that leaves you breathless for more.

Blue and her husband live in a home filled with laughter and creativity, in Long Island, NY. Both working hard to build the Blue brand and cultivate their love for the arts. Creativity is their family affair.

Wait, there is more to come! You can stay updated with my latest releases, learn more about me the author, and be a part of contests by subscribing to my newsletter at

www.BlueSaffire.com

If you enjoyed My Funny Valentine, I'd love to hear

your thoughts and please feel free to leave a

review. And when you do, please let me

know by emailing me TheBlueSaffire@gmail.com

or leave a comment on Facebook
https://www.facebook.com/BlueSaffireDiaries or Twitter
@TheBlueSaffire

Other books by Blue Saffire

Placed in Best Read Order

Also available….

Legally Bound

Legally Bound 2: Against the Law

Legally Bound 5.5: Legally Unbound

Brothers Black 3: Toby the Protector

Coming Soon...

Brothers Black 4: Braxton the Charmer

Brothers Black 5: Felix the Brain

Brothers Black 6: Ryan the Joker

Brothers Black 7: Johnathan the Fixer

Other books from the Evei Lattimore Collection Books by Blue Saffire

Black Bella 1

Destiny 1: Life Decisions

Destiny 2: Decisions of the Next Generation

Destiny 3 coming soon

Made in the USA
Middletown, DE
03 May 2019